"Congratula... It's A Girl."

She looked at John, and he held her baby up like a prize won at a county fair.

"She's gorgeous," he said. "Just like her mother."

"A girl," Annie crooned. She'd given birth, and now she'd never be alone again. She had a family. A daughter.

It all felt so wonderful. So...*right*. Yesterday she hadn't even known this man existed. And now...oh, she couldn't imagine *not* knowing him.

"You're amazing," he said, and she saw admiration and wonder in his eyes. "*She's* amazing."

Annie reached up and caught his hand with hers and said quietly, "Thank you." She wanted to tell him so much. To let him know what it had meant to her that he was there. *"Thank you."*

He shook his head, bent down, kissed her forehead, then kissed the baby. Smiling at Annie, he said, "Annie, I wouldn't have missed this for anything. Thank *you* for letting me witness a miracle."

Dear Reader,

Welcome to the world of Silhouette Desire, where you can indulge yourself every month with romances that can only be described as passionate, powerful and provocative!

The always fabulous Elizabeth Bevarly offers you May's MAN OF THE MONTH, so get ready for *The Temptation of Rory Monahan.* Enjoy reading about a gorgeous professor who falls for a librarian busy reading up on how to catch a man!

The tantalizing Desire miniseries TEXAS CATTLEMAN'S CLUB: LONE STAR JEWELS concludes with *Tycoon Warrior* by Sheri WhiteFeather. A Native American ex-military man reunites with his estranged wife on a secret mission that renews their love.

Popular Peggy Moreland returns to Desire with a romance about a plain-Jane secretary who is in love with her *Millionaire Boss.* The hero-focused miniseries BACHELOR BATTALION by Maureen Child continues with *Prince Charming in Dress Blues,* who's snowbound in a cabin with an unmarried woman about to give birth! *Baby at His Door* by Katherine Garbera features a small-town sheriff, a beautiful stranger and the bundle of love who unites them. And Sara Orwig writes a lovely tale about a couple entering a marriage of convenience in *Cowboy's Secret Child.*

This month, Silhouette is proud to announce we've joined the national campaign "Get Caught Reading" in order to promote reading in the United States. So set a good example, and get caught reading all six of these exhilarating Desire titles!

Enjoy!

Joan Marlow Golan

Joan Marlow Golan
Senior Editor, Silhouette Desire

Please address questions and book requests to:
Silhouette Reader Service
U.S.: 3010 Walden Ave., P.O. Box 1325, Buffalo, NY 14269
Canadian: P.O. Box 609, Fort Erie, Ont. L2A 5X3

Prince Charming in Dress Blues

MAUREEN CHILD

Silhouette® Desire

Published by Silhouette Books
America's Publisher of Contemporary Romance

SILHOUETTE BOOKS

ISBN 0-373-76366-2

PRINCE CHARMING IN DRESS BLUES

Visit Silhouette at www.eHarlequin.com

Printed in U.S.A.

MAUREEN CHILD

was born and raised in Southern California and is the only person she knows who longs for an occasional change of season. She is delighted to be writing for Silhouette Books and is especially excited to be a part of the Desire line.

An avid reader, Maureen looks forward to those rare rainy California days when she can curl up and sink into a good book. Or two. When she isn't busy writing, she and her husband of twenty-five years like to travel, leaving their two grown children in charge of the neurotic golden retriever who is the *real* head of the household. Maureen is also an award-winning historical writer under the names of Kathleen Kane and Ann Carberry.

To My Own Prince Charming, my husband Mark.
Thanks for nearly thirty wonderful years.
I love you more today than I did in '71.

One

"**O**kay," Annie Foster said aloud, "maybe this wasn't such a great idea after all."

The wind snatched her words and threw them off into the surrounding forest. Snow flurries fluttered in that same wind and pelted her face with icy fingers. She blinked and tipped her head back to look at the sky. But there were no stars. Just a wide canvas of black from which more and more snow was falling.

A curl of anxiety unwound in the pit of her stomach and, as if in reaction, the baby in her womb gave her a hard kick.

"Hey," she said, stopping long enough to pat her tummy. "I'm on *your* side, remember?"

A gust of frigid air shot past her, shoving her toward the cabin, and Annie stumbled along with it, trying to keep her footing. All she'd need would be to fall in the snow. With her center of gravity so far off, she'd lie there like an overturned turtle, unable to right herself. Come springtime, some unsuspecting hiker would find her frozen body and she'd make headlines. Hugely Pregnant Woman Fell and Couldn't Get Up.

She laughed shortly at the thought, then continued on toward the cabin. All she could think about now was the warmth inside. Escape from the cold wind and the snow flurries that had been getting steadily thicker for the past hour. Who would have guessed that it would snow so hard in southern California? Well, all right, the *mountains* of southern California. But still. Who worries about snowstorms in a state where a sweatshirt is considered a winter coat?

At the foot of the steps leading to the porch she stopped and cocked her head, listening. A steady, rhythmic pounding carried just under the howl of the wind. Like the heartbeat of some giant snow monster, it seemed to be coming from everywhere and nowhere. It surrounded her, and Annie turned in a slow circle, letting her gaze sweep the edge of the treeline, searching. But there was nothing. Just the swirling snow and the shadowy forest beyond.

She shivered and hunched deeper into her down jacket as she grabbed hold of the banister with one hand and her suitcase with the other. A twinge of discomfort rippled along her back as she climbed the steps slowly, and she hardly winced. After all, she'd been pregnant for eight months now. She was an old hand at this. Used to the occasional spasm or stitch in her side. The infrequent jolt of pain that shot down from her hips all the way to the soles of her feet.

"Pregnancy's not for sissies," she muttered.

Plus, the baby seemed so much bigger in the last few days. Her belly had taken on a life of its own. Heck, it felt as if she was lugging around a small planet. Annie paused halfway up the stairs to take a breath and arch her back, stretching out whatever muscle was kinking. Then, before she could chicken out and just set up camp on the steps, she plodded on, unconsciously keeping time with the eerie pounding still reverberating in the air.

She crossed the porch, opened the door and stepped into a welcoming warmth that almost had her weeping with pleasure.

"Thanks, Lisa," she said in a whispered prayer of gratitude to the friend who had loaned her the cabin for the weekend. Lisa must have called someone and had them turn on the heat so the place would be warm for Annie's arrival. "A true friend," she said as she trudged across the room, still carrying her suitcase.

She could have dropped it in the living room, but Annie was a firm believer in "a place for everything and everything in its place." Besides, she'd only have to move it again later. Might as well get it over with.

When she was halfway down the hall, that twinge in her back came again, only this time it was just a bit stronger. Annie winced, stretched and as she stepped into the bedroom, glanced longingly at the quilt covered king-size bed. A veritable *ocean* of mattress called to her, silently offering a comfy spot for a nap. Dozens of plump pillows in varied shapes and colors were strewn against the headboard, and suddenly all Annie could think of was sinking down into them.

She'd wanted this weekend to be a quiet time. Two days all to herself. To think. To work. To mentally prepare for the coming birth.

Every muscle in her body screamed with fatigue. She'd spent the past six months working herself into a frenzy, trying to prepare for her coming baby. Trying to get ready to be a single mom. Trying to, she told herself tiredly, put the baby's father behind her and think of him only as a kindly sperm donor.

For that's all he really was, anyway. Mike Sinclair. A man of a million promises and a million and a half excuses for breaking them. But she hadn't seen him for what he was. She'd had stars in her eyes that had blinded her to reality. She'd thought he was *The One*. The love of her life. The man she would marry. So she'd turned in her membership card to Virgins Anonymous and slept with him. A few weeks later she'd discovered she was pregnant. When she told Mike...she'd discovered just how fast a human male could really run.

"So he was a mistake," she said, pushing thoughts of the handsome charmer out of her mind as she talked to the mound that was her baby. "At least he gave me you," she said, "and for that I'll always be grateful.

"However," she continued with a sigh, "you do make Mommy tired." Annie set her suitcase down beside the old, hand-carved mahogany dresser, then moved to the bed. Sitting on the edge of the mattress, she clumsily leaned forward and tried to take her shoes off. She managed the right one but gave up on the left. Leaning back, she lifted her feet onto the bed and promised herself she'd wash Lisa's quilt before leaving. Then she eased into those pillows, closed her eyes and drifted off, despite the nagging pain in her back. Twenty-seven years old and she felt like ninety.

* * *

Gunnery Sergeant John Paretti swung the ax high and brought it down with a thud into the log standing upright on an old tree stump. The ax blade bit deeply into the wood, and he pried the two halves apart with gloved hands. Then he split the halves again and again, before gathering up the kindling and tossing it onto the pile he'd already chopped.

By the look of the coming storm, he was going to need all the firewood he could get his hands on. Tipping his head back, he stared up into the wash of white that was now blanketing the sky and the surrounding trees. It had blown up fast, this storm. Rushing across the mountaintop on a freight train of frigid air that stole his breath then turned it into fog in front of his face.

He should have known better, he told himself in disgust as he reached for another log and set it into place on the stump. Should have gone to a beach house to do his thinking. Somewhere down the mountain the February sun was shining, and tourists and locals alike were strolling along the beach walk wearing shorts and sandals. Instead he was dressed like Nanook of the North and frantically chopping firewood to stave off a surprise blizzard.

"Only in California," he muttered and slammed the ax down again.

He'd been working on the woodpile for the last

hour, though to be fair, he probably wouldn't need all of the extra wood. First Sergeant Pete Jackson had promised him when he'd loaned John the cabin that there was a pyramid of firewood ready and waiting. And there was. But between the coming storm and John's own need to work off some of the frustration nearly choking him, he'd decided to chop more.

It was the most recent phone call from his father that had sent him looking for a retreat. As he splintered the wood with sure, strong strokes, he replayed that conversation in his mind.

"Your brothers are married," Dominick Paretti said flatly. "They're settled. They're not going to be leaving the Corps, so it's up to you."

John shook his head and tightened his grip on the receiver. They'd been through this dozens of times. Ever since the old man had resigned from the Corps to start up a small business that had grown into Paretti Computer Corporation, he'd been after his sons to join him. But unlike the old man, his sons were Marines to the bone. And not one of them wanted to give up the Corps to ride a desk and attend board—or as they thought of them, *bored*—meetings.

"Dad," John started, but his father interrupted him quickly.

"Look, John, I'm not getting any younger, you

know?'' The old man's voice roughened up like sandpaper across a stone. ''I want my family to run this business. It's *Paretti* Computers and a Paretti should be in charge when I die.''

''You're not gonna die tomorrow, Dad, and—''

''Think about it,'' his father said, cutting off a possible refusal. ''That's all I ask.''

But, John thought now as he gathered up the firewood and carried it to the porch that ran along the back of the cabin, that wasn't all his dad asked. It never was. He wanted at least one of his three sons to leave the Marines and take over the family business. And he wasn't above using guilt to get his way. The old man, despite his words to the contrary, would go on forever. This had nothing to do with his age or infirm health—the man was healthy as two mules and just as stubborn—this came down to one thing.

Family Comes First.

The Paretti family motto. He and his brothers had been raised to believe that nothing was more important than family. And now Dominick Paretti was counting on his youngest son to live up to what he'd been taught.

Which was why John had borrowed the cabin from Pete for the weekend. He'd needed a place to think. Some quiet time to himself to decide which direction his life should take. Did he go with his heart and stay with the Corps? Or did he go with his head and be the son his father needed?

Wind shrieked across the clearing and shoved him into the log wall behind him. Ducking his head to avoid most of the flying snow, John stared out at the still-whitening world and wondered how the weathermen had missed predicting this storm. He'd been in blizzards before and he recognized the signs. In the last hour, enough snow had fallen to block the driveway and probably the road down the mountain, as well. And it was only going to get worse. Trees bent nearly in half as they surrendered to the wind. Windowpanes rattled behind him, and the lamplight flickered uncertainly. Power lines would be going down next, he told himself and grabbed up an armful of wood before turning for the door.

He stomped into the mudroom, shaking most of the snow off his boots before entering the tiny room off the kitchen. Then, walking straight through the cabin to the living room, he went down on one knee and dropped the load of wood onto the river stone hearth.

"Who's there?" A distinctly female voice called out.

John swiveled on the ball of his foot and shot a glance at the darkened hall and the bedroom beyond. *Who the heck?* He stood up and crossed the room, tugging at the zipper of his jacket as he went. The heater in the small cabin was still on high, and he felt as if he'd parachuted out of the North Pole into the mouth of hell.

"Who is it?" she yelled again, and this time he heard a thread of panic in her voice.

Well, she had a right to be worried. Setting up camp in someone else's cabin. What? Did she think he was running a motel?

Of course, a cynical voice within warned, it could be a trap. Some woman sounding scared to lure him in so her boyfriend could beat him to a pulp and rob him. As that thought settled in, he told himself he'd watched too many movies. Still, it paid to be careful.

Stalking down the short hall, he stopped outside the open bedroom door and carefully poked his head around the corner. He had just enough time to duck as one of the bedside lamps sailed across the room at him.

"Hey!" he shouted above the crash of breaking glass as it hit the wall.

"Stay back!" she ordered. "I have a gun!"

"Then why'd you throw a lamp?"

"I don't want to hurt you if I don't have to."

Real comforting, he thought, with a glance at the shards of broken glass on the floor behind him. Keeping his voice low, calm, he said, "Lady, I don't know what you're doing here, but you'd better go now.''

''*I* should go?'' she echoed, astonishment evident in her tone. ''*You're* the intruder here and—''

Her voice broke off on a gasp and John risked sticking his head back into the danger zone to see what the trouble was. One look was all it took.

''Oh, hell,'' he muttered grimly.

Two

"Are you alone?" he asked.

"I *was*," she said, then winced. Stupid. She never should have told him that. Should have said her big, burly, football-playing husband and eight of his biggest friends were in the next room. Too late now.

"You're pregnant," he said.

"You're a genius," she muttered, and reached toward the table. Keeping one eye on him, she fumbled for something else to throw at him.

She'd come out of a fretful sleep to the sounds of someone crashing around in the living room. Fear had shot through her but was quickly swamped by an almost overpowering sense of protectiveness. She would defend herself—and her baby—with everything she had. Even if that was only—she spared a glance at her arsenal—a paperback novel, a pad of paper and a cordless phone.

Oh, God.

Pitiful.

Annie snatched up the phone, reared her arm back to throw it and stopped when he held up both hands, palms out, toward her.

"Cease fire," he told her.

"Why should I?"

"Because you might hit me."

"That's the point." Really, she'd never expected a burglar to be so chatty. Or so handsome. She mentally erased that thought. His looks had nothing to do with his personality. Weren't there mobsters once known as Pretty Boy Floyd and Baby Face Nelson?

"Look, lady," he said, slowly dropping his arms.

She lifted the phone higher, and his arms shot right back up.

"Okay, okay." He shook his head. "Relax, all right? I'm not going to hurt you."

"If you *were* going to hurt me, would you admit it?" she asked.

"I guess not," he admitted. "But that doesn't change the truth."

She hoped he was telling the truth, because frankly, she just couldn't see herself holding him off much longer. The pains in her back were quickening, and she was fast running out of ammunition, anyway. But how to know whether to trust him or not? How could she be sure that he wouldn't hurt her and her baby?

His eyes, she thought, studying those pale-blue depths that held neither threat nor shadows. She'd always prided herself on being a good judge of character. And those were good eyes. Not necessarily *kind,* but definitely good.

But even as she thought about lowering her weapon, she reminded herself that she'd once looked into Mike Sinclair's eyes and hadn't seen him for the rat he was.

"I don't know what you're doing here," he was saying, "but the guy who owns this place is a friend of mine and—"

Aha! she thought, ignoring the flash of pain down low in her back. Now she had him. "What's his name?" she asked, her gaze narrowing in suspicion.

"Whose name?"

"The owner." Annie scooted back farther against the headboard, knocking a tumble of pillows to the floor. "You see, *I* happen to know the owner, so I'll know if you're lying."

Slowly, carefully, John lowered his hands to his

sides, and when she didn't threaten him, he drew a deep breath. Tilting his head to one side, he looked at her and asked, "And how do I know that? If I tell you his name, you'll just say you knew it, anyway."

"Unless you're lying."

"I don't lie," he said, and leaned one shoulder against the doorjamb.

A Boy Scout intruder. Though he looked incredibly relaxed and calm for a burglar. And that fact irritated Annie more than she could say. Frowning, she said, "Fine. We'll each say the owner's name at the same time."

A short laugh shot from his throat. "What is this? Second grade?"

She ignored that. "On the count of three. One…two…three."

"Peter."

"Lisa."

They stared at each other. As the reality of what must have happened sunk in, Annie asked, "Peter loaned you the cabin?"

"Yep," he said, nodding. "And Lisa did the same for you?"

"Oh, for heaven's sake."

Another, sharper pain poked at her spine, and Annie winced as she sat up and swung her legs off the edge of the bed. Shooting him a long look, she said, "Well, Peter obviously made a mistake, and you should go."

"I was here first."

"Now who's in second grade?" she demanded.

"Lady…"

"And stop calling me *lady* in that tone."

"What tone?"

One blond eyebrow lifted into a high arch. "That tone that says, 'calm down crazy person.'"

He frowned and straightened away from the door. "That's not what I meant."

She winced as another ripple of pain unwound inside her, this time rolling from the base of her spine all the way around her immense belly and back again. *Not now,* she silently pleaded with the baby. For pity's sake, give Mommy a break.

John took half a step forward and stopped dead. She still didn't trust him, he knew, so she wouldn't want him offering to catch her when she fainted.

And she was going to faint, he thought. Or worse. His mouth dried up and his throat tightened. He'd watched a wave of pain overtake her. Could actually *see* it grabbing her, tensing her body. Her small, oval-shaped face went so white her pale-blond eyebrows actually stood out in sharp relief against their colorless background.

His gaze dropped briefly to her swollen belly, and John frantically wished himself into the middle of a firefight somewhere. Hell, he'd take flying bullets, exploding mortars and hand grenades anyday…anything had to be better than being stuck in a tiny cabin with a woman about to go into labor.

Just thinking the word *labor* sent his stomach on a sharp plunge to his feet. At last he understood the expression *a sinking feeling.* It was kind of like stepping unknowingly into the La Brea Tar Pits. Every move you made only sucked you in deeper. There was no escape. Just the inevitable. The only question was, how long would it take you to go down?

"Are you all right?" he asked, hoping to God she'd say, Sure. Just a little toothache.

"Do I *look* all right?" she asked, lifting her head long enough to slide him a glare that should have toasted him on the spot.

"Actually," he said, with an inward sigh, "no."

Her lips twisted into a mocking smile. "Gee, thanks."

Then she groaned and clapped one hand to her middle.

All the air left John's lungs.

"C'mon, sweetie," she murmured, smoothing one hand up and down over her stomach, "not now, okay?"

"It's labor, isn't it?" he asked when he'd managed to suck more air into his body.

She laughed shortly. "Well, I've never done this before, so I can't be sure, but yeah. That's my guess. I've been having a backache all day but the pain seems to be coming every few minutes now."

"Swell."

The little blonde shot him a bland look. "Gee, I'm sorry to inconvenience you."

Shame swamped him. Here he was thinking about himself, when this woman was about to make a new human being. Well, hell, you couldn't blame a guy, could you? He'd come to this cabin for a little peace and quiet. Not to be the first Marine midwife in history.

"I think you should take me to the closest hospital," she said, scooting carefully off the bed.

If only he could. "There's a problem."

"Problem?" she echoed as she tried to slip her right foot back into a sadly misshapen loafer.

"We're not going anywhere," he said and watched realization dawn on her face with each of his words. Damn, it cost him to break this to her, but better she know straight-out that *he* was as close to a doctor as she'd be seeing tonight. God help her.

"What do you mean?"

"I mean, the storm has turned into a blizzard. There are drifts of snow blocking the driveway, and I'm pretty sure the roads are in no better shape."

Her blue eyes widened, and she shot a quick look at the nearest window. Outside, the wind hammered at the glass like an angry old man demanding entry.

"Well, find a snowplow."

"I don't have one."

"What kind of mountain cabin doesn't have a snow plow?"

Pointless to wish for things they didn't have, he thought. "I'll mention it to Pete next time I see him." Along with a few other things, like making sure the cabin was unoccupied *before* you lent it out.

"There can't be a blizzard," she said, interrupting his thoughts and swinging her gaze back to him. "I'm having a baby."

Oh, man. He forced a smile he didn't feel and told himself she didn't need to see just how nervous she was making him. The thought of becoming an instant obstetrician didn't exactly electrify him. But what choice did he have? Hell, what choice did *either* of them have? That baby was coming whether they liked it or not.

And in this situation the baby had the last word.

"Maybe we could call for help," she said, waving the phone she still held in one hand.

"Good idea," he said and cursed silently for not thinking of it himself.

"I'll call 911," she said to herself as she turned

the phone on and dialed. "This is an emergency, right?"

"Oh, yeah, I'd say so," he told her. Heck, if he had any rocket flares, he'd be firing them about now.

She held the phone up to her ear, and he watched eagerness fade into disbelief and then fear.

"What?" he asked, not really wanting to hear her answer.

"It's not working."

"What do you mean it's not working?" he asked, reaching for the phone.

"It's not dialing."

He took it, listened for a long minute, hoping the situation would change, then gave it up. That sinking sensation crawled back into his guts and he wondered if it was going to become a permanent part of him. "The phone's dead."

"Oh, God."

"Don't worry," he said, and instantly told himself how stupid *that* was. Of course she'd worry. She was probably terrified. Having a baby during a blizzard, with the only help available a complete stranger? Those wide blue eyes of hers shone with a glimmer of unshed tears and just a trace of dread. Hell, he was just short of panicking himself. But even as that thought registered, he put it aside. Marines don't panic, for God's sake. Marines fight battles. And Marines *win*, by damn.

She licked dry lips and gave him a quick, frantic glance. "Maybe it's not labor. Maybe it's gas."

"You really think so?"

"No," she said, shaking her head and rubbing her mouth with her fingertips. "Just wishful thinking. Oh, God," she added in a soft, panic filled murmur, "what am I going to do?"

"We can do this," he said, making sure his voice sounded firm but comforting.

"*We* can?" she asked, grabbing the phone from him and shaking it as if she could bring it back to life.

"I'll help any way I can."

She kept shaking the phone.

He took it from her and set it back into the cradle. "Shaking it won't help. The line must have gone down."

"The power line?" she asked.

"No," he said with a grateful look at the lamplight, "power's still on. I don't know for how long, though."

"This is *not* happening," she whispered, and sank down onto the edge of the bed.

"Yeah," John said quietly, "it is." Though he wished to hell it wasn't.

She shot him a quick look. "I had this planned, you know."

"You *planned* this?" He took a seat beside her.

Unbelievably enough, a short laugh shot from her throat. "No, I didn't plan *this*. I planned how it would be when the baby came."

John just looked at her. "You can plan that stuff?"

She nodded, more to herself than to him. "You just have to be organized, is all." She glanced at him and went on. "At home, I have the doctor's number by the phone, my packed suitcase by the front door and the baby's layette all pressed and ready."

"That's a plan," he said, and told himself she'd make a halfway decent General.

She folded her hands in what was left of her lap and entwined her fingers. "This isn't how I thought it would be. I thought I'd be in the hospital. With nurses. With doctors. With *medication*."

Her voice notched up a bit higher with every word, and he felt the tension inside her escalate. He had to keep her calm. Hysteria wasn't going to help either of them through this.

"But I'm stuck here. In a cabin. With—" she looked at him. "I don't even know your name."

"John," he told her, offering his right hand. "John Paretti."

Her bottom lip trembled a bit, and that hit him harder than he would have expected.

She took his hand and said, "Annie. Annie Foster."

"Nice to meet you."

"Yeah," she said, and her mouth quirked into a mocking smile. "I'll bet. You're probably wishing you were out in that blizzard somewhere."

"Nope," he said, and surprised himself by meaning it. If he wasn't here, she'd be alone. And he didn't like the thought of that at all. Better that he was here. Not that he knew what the hell to do, but at least she wasn't alone. At least he could be another heartbeat in the cabin. "There's nowhere else I'd rather be at this moment."

"Really?" she asked, and this time she gave him a genuine smile that hit him like a hard fist to his midsection. "I can think of at least a dozen places I'd rather be."

"Can't say as I blame you any," John said, "but try not to worry."

"Don't *worry?*"

"Well, okay," he said, keeping his voice low and soft, "I guess you'll worry, anyway. But the point is, at least you're not alone. We'll get through this."

She reached up and pushed one hand through her short cap of blond curls, "*We* will, huh?"

John gave her another smile he hoped looked more convincing than it felt and reached for her hand. "Sure. How hard can it be? People have been having babies for centuries."

"Yeah," she murmured, "and I wish some of them were here right now." He smiled, appreciating a woman who could make jokes when things looked black. "Oh, no…here's another one…." Then she grabbed at him, curling her fingers into his forearm until each one of her nails dug through the fabric of his jacket and the shirt beneath, to bite into his skin. Man, she had a helluva grip.

Misery shimmered across her features. Her lips clamped tightly shut, she breathed quickly, deeply through her nose and closed her eyes as she rode the wave of pain gripping her.

John had never felt so helpless in his life.

Not knowing what else to do, he smoothed his free hand up and down her back in long, comforting strokes. And even through the thick, blue cable-knit sweater she wore, he felt her muscles tighten convulsively.

"Are you okay?" Dumb question, Paretti, he told himself as her fingernails slowly eased back out of his skin. She trembled, and he wanted to pick her up and carry her bodily through the snow. Find a hospital. Find a doctor who could give her something to ease the pain. A doctor who could take care of her and her baby.

And he couldn't do it. All he could offer her was a shoulder to cry on and the promise that he wouldn't leave her.

A long, deep breath shuddered into her lungs before she looked up at him. An invisible fist clutched at his heart, squeezing painfully. Sapphire-blue eyes stared back at him, and John saw fear and hope, and unbelievably enough, *excitement* shining in those vivid depths.

"That one was much stronger," she told him. "I think the baby's going to be here soon."

He buried the knot of panic swelling inside him and said only, "Then let's get ready to greet it."

Three

The night crawled on.

She'd been wrong. The baby hadn't been as close as she'd thought. Minutes were measured in soft moans that tore at John even as he admired the woman who refused to cry out despite the pain that kept blossoming inside her. He knew it was far worse now. He saw the advancement of the pain on her face. Her features tightened, draining her of color. Her blond hair lay damp against her forehead, and those lake-blue eyes of hers were glassy with concentration and agony.

And there wasn't a damn thing he could do to help her.

Helplessness was not something he was used to feeling. Until tonight there'd never been a problem he couldn't solve. A situation he couldn't take charge of. As a man—a Marine—he'd prided himself on being able to handle whatever came his way. It was second nature to him to offer help. To fix whatever was broken.

But now, despite his training, despite wishing things were different, he was nothing more than a bystander. All he could do was watch as Mother Nature did what she did best.

And damned if he wasn't humbled.

As the latest pain faded away, John watched her breathe easier, saw the tension leave her body and was probably more grateful than she for the respite.

"Oh, my," she whispered and swallowed hard. "That was a hard one."

He was suddenly aware that his hands were curled into tight fists. Deliberately he relaxed them and walked to her side. Picking up a damp washcloth, he wiped her forehead, smoothing her soft blond hair back and accepting her smile with all the pride he would have a medal.

"Thanks," she said and pulled in one or two deep breaths. "This is a heck of a first impression I make, don't you think?"

John smiled down at her. "It's not a night I'm likely to forget."

"Me, neither," she assured him and rubbed one hand across the mound of her child. "But then, when this is over, I'll have my baby."

He watched her hand move slowly, tenderly, and not for the first time he noticed the lack of a wedding ring. Did that mean she wasn't married? Or that her rings didn't fit anymore? Hadn't he heard his own mother complain about being pregnant with him and his brothers and how she hadn't been able to wear her wedding rings for the swelling?

Probably shouldn't say anything, he thought, but at the same time, if she was *his* wife, he'd be terrified at the thought of her stuck in a blizzard. Of course, if she had been his wife, she wouldn't have been traveling alone so close to the birth of their baby.

Taking a seat beside her on the mattress, he asked, "Is there anyone who's going to be worried about you?" And even as the words left his mouth, he thought, Oh, nice job, Paretti. Could you make her sound more alone?

She pushed herself a little higher against the pillows and shook her head. "If you mean, do I have a husband somewhere pacing the floor, the answer is no."

"I didn't mean to—"

"Pry?" she finished for him, and gave him a tired smile. "John, you *undressed* me and put me to bed. Before the night's over, you're going to deliver my baby. I don't think a question is out of line.''

He still felt like an idiot.

"And, as I said, the answer is no," she said in a voice pitched so low he had to strain to hear it. "No husband. No anxious father. It's just me. And the baby.''

"I'm sorry,'' he said. "It's none of my business.''

"Probably not,'' she agreed, "but don't be sorry for me. It's an old story, certainly not a new one. I picked a lemon in the garden of love.'' Her hand on her belly paused, as if she were trying to keep the baby from hearing what she was about to say. "When he found out I was pregnant, he left.''

Okay, now he knew who the *real* idiot was. "Stupid of him,'' he said.

Annie smiled at the compliment. "Thanks. I thought so.'' Really, as "burglars'' went, he was a very nice man. And she was more grateful than she could say that he was there. She didn't even want to imagine what it would have been like to be stranded, alone and giving birth. She squirmed a bit on the bed, feeling the pad of towels John had folded and slipped beneath the sheet. She just couldn't get comfortable, she thought, and briefly longed again for that fabulous epidural she'd heard other women talking about. Funny how this had worked out. She'd never had any intention of having a natural childbirth. Annie was a big believer in taking advantage of medical science. After all, a hundred years ago women were putting knives under the bed to "cut the pain." Who was she to go without medication when people had worked for years to make childbirth easier, safer and pain free?

Something inside her began the slow, unmistakable tightening that by now she recognized all too well. Another contraction was coming. Her body readied for that slow climb to agony. And since there was no anesthetist around to give her a hand, she settled for something else.

"Talk to me," she whispered as her insides tightened and her back arched as she moved into the pain.

His eyes widened. "About what?"

"Anything," she assured him. She just wanted something else to concentrate on besides her own discomfort. "Tell me about your family. Are you married?"

He laughed shortly and shook his head. "Me? No. I figure I'll stay single and save some poor woman a lot of headaches."

Oh, it was a big one. She tried to ride the wave, told herself that with each pain, her baby was that much closer. Keep talking, she thought. "Scared, huh?"

John's head jerked back, and he looked at her. "Scared? Who said anything about scared?"

Despite her distress she laughed at his offended tone, then gasped and reached for his hands. Holding on tightly, she only said, "Talk, John. Talk to me."

"Uh," he said, letting his gaze sweep over her before settling back on her face, "I have two brothers. They've both gotten married recently. Nice women," he muttered, words tumbling out of his mouth, and she clung to each one as if it were a tiny life raft. "Can't figure out why they'd want to be married to Nick or Sam, but, hey, I never did understand women."

A twist of her lips was the best smile she could give him. "So few do," she said, and panted for air. "Tell me about them. About you."

"We're Marines," he said, throwing the words out quickly. "All of us."

Not a Boy Scout after all, she told herself, but close.

"More," she said through gritted teeth, seeing the pain as a red haze that settled over her eyes, blurring the rest of the world until only his voice kept her anchored.

"My brother Sam is stationed in South Carolina.

He just married a woman named Karen. She's a real estate agent. Nice lady. Keeps Sam hopping, I can tell you.''

Her hands tightened on his.

John spoke quickly, keeping the words flowing.

''Nick, he's stationed here. At Camp Pendleton, like me. He's married to Gina.'' John laughed shortly, and she clung to the sound of it. ''She's Italian, too, so the two of them together get pretty loud when there's a difference of opinion. But Nick—hell, he's a marshmallow when it comes to her.''

Calm, deliberate, he kept talking, telling her about his family, drawing her into his life. And as he talked, she listened, getting to know him not just through his words but through the gentle touch of his hands and the quiet timbre of his voice. While the wind howled outside and her body screamed inside, her mind reached out for him and held on.

''Okay,'' John told her from his position at the foot of the bed, ''I think this is it.''

He'd drawn on every bit of medical training he'd ever received in the Corps to help him out during the last several hours. And, God knew, it hadn't been much. Knowing how to tie a bandage or temporarily set a broken bone wasn't going to get him far tonight. But at least he felt somewhat prepared for what was coming.

John only hoped he wouldn't screw this up. Let her down. He was all she had to count on now. All the baby had to count on.

His heart ached to watch her writhing in a pain she refused to acknowledge. She was either the bravest or the stubbornest woman he'd ever known. He knew damn well she was in agony, yet she'd hardly made a peep all night. Hell, he'd seen Marines wailing over a flesh wound. But Annie had simply gritted her teeth, steeled her will and ridden the pain out.

Through it all, she'd amazed him with her courage.

And now that the payoff was here…the birth imminent…he only hoped he measured up to her.

"Get set, Annie. Next time you feel like it, you give this baby a big push into the world."

Annie nodded, propped herself up onto her elbows, took a deep breath and clenched her jaw. Every muscle in her body tightened, preparing for battle. When an overwhelming compulsion took hold, she pushed with everything she had, concentrating on moving her baby from her womb into her waiting arms.

"'Atta girl," John said, and she heard him as if

from a distance. "Keep going, don't stop now. It's coming. I can see its head."

A smile bubbled up inside her, despite the pain roaring through her body. Almost, she told herself. Almost. After all these months, the moment was finally here.

"Breathe, Annie," he ordered, "you've got to breathe. Take a breath for God's sake."

She sucked in air, used it for ammunition and bore down again. How many times, she wondered, her mind racing at a wild speed, had she seen this scene on television? Or in the movies? *Push, push,* someone was always shouting, and the poor beleaguered woman always ended up crying out, "I can't."

Well, not Annie. She felt as though she couldn't *stop* pushing. Her body had a mind of its own now. She was just along for the ride. Nature had stepped in and there was no stopping it. And as suddenly as that thought came, John called out, "Okay, ease back a little now. Stop pushing for a minute."

"No way," she muttered. Her eyes flew open, and she looked at him where he knelt between her up-drawn legs. No modesty left, she thought idly, not caring right now *who* saw her in the most humiliating position a woman could find herself in. All she wanted now was to get this baby *out.*

The urge to push clawed at her. "Have to," she

said between gasps for air, "have to push. Have to do it now."

"I know, honey," he said, his voice soft, his hands against her body gentle. Then he met her gaze and gave her a smile. "The baby's head's out and it's turning, so just hold back a minute or two more. It knows what to do, all we have to do is give it time to do it."

She blew air out in short, sharp puffs and told herself to hang on. Just another minute. And finally, when she thought she couldn't stand it a second longer, she heard him say, "All right Annie, let's meet this baby."

"Thank God," she moaned and put everything she had into one last, colossal effort to push her child from her body.

"Scream if you want to, honey," he told her in a loud, clear voice. "No one's around to hear you."

She didn't want to scream. Didn't want to waste that much breath. But as she felt her body give and stretch and pull taut, Annie heard a high, keening wail splinter the air and it wasn't until much later that she realized the sound had come from her.

The baby cried and Annie laughed, falling back against the pillows like a runner exhausted after a marathon.

John's voice, so familiar, so comforting, carried above the infant's outraged screech. "It's a girl,

Annie,'' he said, pleasure and awe coloring his tone.

She looked at him and he held her baby up like a prize won in a county fair.

"She's gorgeous," he said. "Just like her mother."

"A girl," Annie crooned, lifting her arms out for the messy, squalling baby whose tiny arms and legs kicked furiously.

"Let me just clean her up a little," he said with a wink.

So tired, Annie thought as she nodded and closed her eyes. She'd never been more tired. Or more fulfilled. She'd done it. She'd given birth and now she'd never be alone again. She had a family. A daughter.

One part of her mind listened as John moved around the room, tending to the baby, talking to her.

"You caused quite a stir, young lady," he was saying, and the baby's cries quieted, matching his soft tone. "Your mommy's tired now, and I'm going to be a little busy seeing to her, so I want you to just take it easy and let her rest for a bit, all right?"

Annie chuckled under her breath. It all felt so wonderful. So...*right*. Yesterday she hadn't even known this man existed. And now...oh, she thought as he came toward her and laid her brand-new baby in her arms, now she couldn't imagine *not* knowing him.

As she tucked the squirming bundle of her daughter close to her side, Annie felt John's fingers trace delicately across her forehead. She tore her gaze from the beautiful sight of her daughter's face to look up at him.

"You're amazing," he said and she saw admiration and wonder in his eyes. "*She's* amazing."

Annie reached up and caught his hand with hers. Unexpected tears filled her eyes as she met his gaze and said quietly, "Thank you."

"You don't have to—"

"No," she said, cutting him off and staring deeply into his eyes. She wanted to tell him so much. To let him know what it had meant to her that he was there. That he was kind. And calm. And gentle. But all she could say was the same two words. "Thank you."

He shook his head, bent down, kissed her forehead, then kissed the baby for good measure. Smiling at Annie, he said, "Annie, I wouldn't have missed this for anything. Thank *you* for letting me witness a miracle."

Four

John leaned one shoulder against the doorjamb and stared at the sleeping woman across the room from him. She looked so small in the big bed, half-buried under a blue-and-white quilt and surrounded by a mountain of pillows.

But he wasn't fooled by her size. He knew first-hand just how tough this woman was.

His insides flipped once, hard. Now that the emergency was over, he could take a minute to fully appreciate just how lucky they'd both been. The baby was a month early, but she was big and healthy. No complications during delivery. No problems at all, really. And as that thought fluttered through his mind, he sent up a quick, heartfelt prayer of gratitude.

The baby, lying in the crook of Annie's arm, stirred and whimpered. John pushed away from the wall and walked quickly, soundlessly to the side of the bed. Shadows of exhaustion lay beneath Annie's eyes, but the baby looked wide-eyed and ready for trouble.

A pair of hazy blue eyes looked up at him, and despite knowing that he probably looked like a big blur to her, John told himself that the tiny girl was staring right at him. One impossibly small hand lifted and long, fragile fingers reached for him. He sucked in a gulp of air and actually *felt* it when the baby's fist closed around his heart.

"A heartbreaker," he whispered, and carefully lifted the baby, still wrapped in her bath-towel blanket, from the circle of Annie's arm. "That's what you are. A heartbreaker."

She only stared at him owlishly.

"Come on, now, let's give your mom some sleep time," he said, his voice taking on an instinctive, singsong rhythm. Cuddling her into his chest, John headed for the main room and surprised himself by just how much he enjoyed the feel of that new life in his arms.

He'd never imagined himself as a father—despite the fact that he'd had a damn near perfect childhood, raised by parents who loved each other. Fatherhood just wasn't something that had appealed to him. Maybe it was the whole idea of being responsible for another human being. Maybe it was fear of screwing up an innocent kid by making stupid parenting mistakes.

But whatever the reason, he'd avoided all chances at a serious relationship that might have led to parenthood. He'd always told himself that he was perfectly happy in his life. Answering to no one but the Corps. Going his own way. Doing his own thing.

But now, he thought as he took a seat on the floor near the fireplace and leaned back against the sofa, he had to wonder. The small, sturdy weight on his arm felt good. Right, somehow. And looking down into a pair of eyes that had seen nothing of the world made him want to show her everything.

She waved her little hand at him again, and this time he caught her fist with his fingertips. Smoothing the pad of his thumb into her closed fist, he felt those little fingers, sensed the strength inside and was humbled all over again.

"You're a booby trap, aren't you?" he asked quietly, and she tilted her head as if trying to understand him. "Yep," he went on, smiling now at the frowns and grimaces tightening her little features. "You look all innocent and everything. But once a person gets close, you suck 'em in and take 'em out.''

She stretched and yawned, obviously bored with the conversation. John chuckled and tucked the towel more closely around her little body. Amazing, really, he thought. Only a few hours ago she wasn't here. And now she was breathing and fussing and making herself known in no uncertain terms. An entire, new person.

And he already loved her with a fierceness he wouldn't have believed possible.

Annie stood in the doorway, watching the two of them. Her heartbeat staggered slightly at the simple beauty of that gorgeous man tenderly holding the baby. Laying one hand against the doorjamb, she steadied her shaky knees and took a long minute to just enjoy the picture in front of her.

She still wasn't sure just who John Paretti was, but she was positive of one thing: tonight he'd been her guardian angel. And as that thought ricocheted through her mind, she told herself he even *looked* like some dark angel. Black hair, pale, icy-blue eyes and a face made up of sharp planes and angles.

Silhouetted by the fire, his profile was strong, and his biceps looked huge even through the fabric of his Irish knit sweater. Yet this powerful-looking man held her newborn daughter with a tenderness she could sense from across the room. And she knew, from firsthand experience, just how gentle those big hands of his could be.

A small curl of embarrassment wound through her before she could stop it. Silly, she thought, with an inward smile. Way too late to be embarrassed now. John had seen every inch of her—and not from a particularly flattering angle.

And now that she thought about it, just what did you say to a man after sharing something like that? How about dinner? Nope. She didn't think so. Besides, no point in getting attached to tall, dark and gorgeous. As soon as the snow cleared up, they'd be going their separate ways. She frowned as a distinct feeling of regret flared up inside her.

Now where did that come from? she wondered, and quickly quashed the notion. But before it was totally gone, he turned his head and looked directly at her as if he was reading her mind and entertained by it.

"Should you be out of bed?"

Annie smiled and lifted one shoulder in a half-hearted shrug. "I couldn't stay in bed." Her gaze drifted from his to her daughter's firelit face. "I got lonely."

"She was fussing, thought I'd let you get some sleep."

Pushing away from the wall, she crossed the

room and carefully...*very* carefully, eased down onto the sofa beside him. "Ridiculous to admit this," she said, wincing slightly as she settled into the cushions, "but I'm not really tired."

Her entire body ached, yet she felt better than she had in years. In fact, she felt completely energized. As if she could run a marathon or climb a mountain or...okay, maybe not. But the least she could do was sit up and talk to the man she owed so much to.

He turned his head and looked up at her, and as the firelight flickered across his features, a feminine dart of admiration shot through her. Really, he was way too good-looking. Then he smiled and her heartbeat skipped a bit.

"I think she's starting to look for dinner."

"Hmm? Oh!" Shaking her head she told herself to get a grip on obviously rampaging hormones, then held out her arms for the baby. John gently handed over her daughter, but didn't move back as Annie tucked the infant into the crook of her arm.

"She's amazing," he whispered, and she felt the brush of his breath across her cheek.

"She really is beautiful, isn't she?" Annie asked, turning her face toward his and almost gasping at just how close he was. Only a breath away. And in a deep corner of her mind Annie realized that if the circumstances were different, she just might be fantasizing about being kissed.

Her gaze dropped briefly to his mouth, and she sucked in air and deliberately looked away. Boy, this hormone thing could really get out of hand.

"So what's her name?" he asked.

The baby. Good. Talk about the baby, keep her mind off his mouth. "Jordan," she said, smiling at the child she'd been waiting forever to meet in person.

"Pretty name."

"Thanks," she said, then added, "and thanks again for what you did for me and Jordan."

"You already thanked me," he said quietly, his voice blending in with the hiss and crackle of the flames just a few feet away.

Not enough, she thought, knowing that a part of her would always be thanking him. For the rest of Jordan's life, Annie would be saying an extra prayer each night for the man who'd seen them both safely through. "Yeah, well, I figure delivering a baby deserves more than just one thank-you."

"Okay," he said, smiling at her again, and one more time she felt that quickening of her heart.

For heaven's sake. She'd just given birth a few hours ago.

"But I ought to be thanking you, too," he pointed out.

She laughed shortly. "For what? Squeezing your hands hard enough to break bones?"

He grinned, and Annie's breath caught. She wondered if he was aware just how lethal a weapon that smile of his was.

"Nope," he said, "though you do have a hell of a grip. I meant for missing me when you threw that lamp."

Annie winced at the memory. "I'm sorry about that, but you did surprise me and—"

"No problem," he said, "I'm just glad you don't have better aim."

"I have great aim," she countered. "Labor pains distracted me."

"For which I'm grateful."

"As it turned out, so am I," she admitted with a wry smile. After all, what would she have done if she'd knocked out her only help?

The baby squirmed restlessly, and Annie stroked one fingertip along her cheek. Jordan turned her head into Mommy's touch, opening and closing her mouth as she blindly searched for food. Annie smiled to herself. This she could do. Even without any of the baby supplies she had waiting at home. "She's hungry," she whispered.

"Looks like," John said, and eased back a little. Then shifting his gaze to hers, he said, "Why don't you feed her, and I'll go fix us something to eat. Give you two some privacy."

One corner of her mouth lifted into a small smile. "It's a little late to be worrying about my modesty, isn't it?"

He actually looked embarrassed as he stood up, shoved his hands into the back pockets of his jeans and looked down at her. "That was different. That was an emergency situation. This is…"

"Dinnertime?" Annie finished for him.

"Exactly," he said, nodding and turning for the kitchen.

As she watched him retreat, Annie smiled to herself. An interesting man, she thought, as she unbuttoned her nightgown and bared her breast. He'd seen her through the most incredible, terrifying night of her life with a sense of calm that had eased her own fears. But he'd run from the sight of her nursing the baby he'd delivered.

Then Jordan's little mouth clamped around her nipple, and Annie's mind emptied. Sensations crowded her, and she hugged every one of them to her: her child's small warm body cuddled close; firelight dancing around the room; the wind driven snow pelting the windowpanes; and the comforting knowledge that John Paretti was in the next room.

It wasn't embarrassment that had chased him out of the room, John thought from the kitchen's shadowy doorway. He'd seen women nurse babies before. Heck, there were enough Paretti cousins to populate a small country. He'd grown up surrounded by nursing women. This was something entirely different.

Something he figured would be best left unidentified.

But a tightening low inside him warned that ignoring it wouldn't make it go away. And not putting a name to it didn't change a damn thing. Ridiculous, he argued silently with himself. All right, so she's beautiful. And strong. And incredibly brave. She also just had a baby. John lifted one hand and scrubbed it hard across his face.

Man, he was some kind of dog, he thought. He had to be. Otherwise, why would he find the sight of Annie breast-feeding her baby so damned erotic? Hell, he'd been alone too long. What he needed was to get back into the dating pool. Find himself a nice, warm body to cozy up to. Unfortunately, the only warm body he was interested in was out there in the main room. And she wouldn't be cozying up to anybody for at least six weeks. Even then, he thought, she probably wouldn't be interested in dating a man who'd already seen her at her most vulnerable.

Probably for the best, he told himself, deliberately turning his back on the private moment Annie was sharing with her new daughter. He moved into the kitchen, opened the pantry door and stared blindly at the mountain of supplies Pete and Lisa kept on hand. Yeah, for the best. He wasn't looking for anything permanent, and a woman who'd just had a child wouldn't be looking for anything temporary.

"Laughing at me is *not* productive."

"I'm not laughing *at* you," John told her around a fresh burst of chuckles, "I'm laughing *with* you."

Sure. She believed that. "Do I look like I'm laughing to you?"

He sobered instantly, then gave it up as his lips twitched again. "Guess not." He took a deep breath. "Sorry."

But he didn't look the least bit apologetic. And if she wasn't feeling so frustrated, she might not have blamed him for laughing. But as it was… Annie huffed out a breath of air, fluttering the bangs on her forehead. Staring down at her still-naked baby and the makeshift diaper she could not, for some reason, make fit, Annie wished futilely for one of those neat little disposable jobs.

But the snow was still blowing outside, as it had been since the night before, so a trip to the local market was out of the question.

"You're getting better," he said in a placating tone.

"You're not a very good liar," she told him on

a sigh. Ordinarily, not a bad trait in a man, she thought. However, right now she could have used a comforting little lie.

"That one really wasn't too bad," John said, and she slid him a long, slow look out of narrowed eyes.

"Gee, thanks." Good-looking, charming and a master with a dishtowel diaper. Was there no end to the man's talents?

"You'll get the hang of it," John assured her, apparently unfazed by her glare. "Just remember that the object of the whole business is to actually *cover* the baby's bottom."

"Very funny," she muttered, and bent to fold the dish towel one more time. Jordan lay still on the bed, blinking her hazy blue eyes at the ceiling as if trying to figure out exactly where she was. Poor little thing. She had no idea that her mother was so helpless, that a Marine made a better mommy.

But she'd improve. Looking down into her daughter's tiny face, Annie promised her that she would learn everything and that she would be the best mom she could possibly be. Maybe Jordan wouldn't have a father around like the other kids, but she would have a mother who would always be there for her.

And with that thought firmly in mind, Annie swallowed her pride, looked up at John and said, "Show me again?"

He smiled at her, and her heart did that strange

little blip again. All right, last night she'd put her reaction to him down to the emotion of the moment, her daughter's birth, the unusual closeness she'd experienced with this man. But now—she couldn't afford to start having warm, fuzzy feelings for a man who would, no doubt, disappear from her life the minute the storm ended. So she'd better just concentrate on the task at hand and forget about that half dimple in his right cheek.

"Sure," he said, splintering her thoughts, for which she was more grateful than he would ever know. John took the halved dish towel, folded it and bent to lift Jordan's legs. He slid the fabric under the baby's fanny, then brought the rest of the material through her little legs and around her waist. "See, it's all in the positioning. Get it square under her little butt, and then keep it taut around her belly when you pin the edges together."

"Pins," Annie muttered, wondering if Lisa had some duct tape somewhere in this cabin. "What if I stick her?"

He turned his head and looked at her. "You won't. Just keep your fingers between the diaper and her skin. If you stick anybody, it'll be yourself."

She nodded, watching his big hands move gently, deftly over the baby's tiny body. When he was finished, he slid those wide palms beneath Jordan, lifted her off the bed and settled her into the crook of Annie's arm.

"There," he said. "All dry. For now," he added wryly.

"She is going through a lot of Lisa's towels," Annie mused, looking from her daughter's wide yawn up to John's blue eyes.

"At least we've got plenty," he said with a quick glance at the window, where snow was piling up along the edge of the sill. "Looks like we're going to be here for a couple more days at least."

"Won't you get in trouble?" Annie asked. "You said you're a Marine. Don't you have to report in or something?"

"I'm on leave," he said, turning back to look at her. "Two more weeks all to myself."

"You're not getting much of a vacation," Annie said and silently decided that his eyes weren't ice blue at all, but the soft blue of a cloudless summer sky.

"Depends on your point of view," he said. "From where I'm sitting, it's not so bad."

Yeah, well, from where she was standing, it looked pretty good, too.

Too good.

Five

There days later the storm had stopped and the sun was shining. John had managed to clear at least part of the driveway, giving him enough room to maneuver his four-wheel-drive monster of a car around from the side of the house. Then he'd headed into the tiny town of Big Bear, where he'd, thank heaven, Annie thought, purchased a supply of disposable diapers and a few other essentials.

He'd also brought a doctor to examine her and the baby. Once they were both pronounced "fit as a fiddle," John had taken the man home.

Now, as she sat across the kitchen table from him, watching him give Jordan a bottle of water, she planted her elbows on the table, propped her chin in her hands and said, "I've got to ask."

One black eyebrow lifted and he glanced at her. "Ask what?"

How did he do that, she wondered. How did he manage to look both sexy and tender at the same time? And when were those stray thoughts going to stop shooting across her mind?

Swallowing hard, she focused on the conversation at hand and said, "How did you get to know so much about babies?"

He continually amazed her. She'd been reading parenting books for eight months, and he just slid into baby mode as if he'd been born for it. Annie'd never really imagined a Marine—a professional *soldier* for pity's sake—as being quite so...domestic.

"Hey," he said, as if it explained everything, "I'm Italian."

"So?" she countered. "I'm Scotch-Irish, and that information along with three bucks will get me a latte. It doesn't qualify me as mother of the year."

His lips curved into that smile she'd come to know and look forward to. Her heart did a curious two step again as she took a moment to just enjoy the view. Honestly, that one dimple of his was just too much for any one female to have to deal with.

"I come from a big family," he said.

"Three sons isn't that big."

"Yeah, but I'm counting cousins, too." He took the bottle from the baby's mouth, and Jordan lay limply in his grasp, her tiny mouth still working furiously. Setting the bottle down, he lifted the baby to his shoulder and gently patted her back. "My dad has four brothers and a sister, and my mom's from a family of seven kids."

Annie quickly did the math and felt her eyebrows arch high on her forehead. "Wow."

"Yeah," he said, "tell me about it. You should have seen us all at Thanksgiving. And Christmas Eve."

"You all got together?" she said, trying to imagine the hubbub created by such a huge gathering of family members. But being the only child of older parents, she really had no basis for comparison. Her holidays were always quiet, dignified celebrations. She and her parents would exchange thoughtful, suitable gifts and then share a meal at whatever restaurant they'd chosen for that year's festivities.

Not that she was complaining, she thought, with more than a twinge of guilt. Her parents had done their best. It was simply that they hadn't counted on being parents. Annie's birth had come as a complete surprise to both of them, since they were at an age when the children of their friends were graduating from high school and entering college. Her parents had looked at the arrival of a baby as they would have a guest showing up three hours after the party ended. She was welcome, but they weren't really sure what to do with her.

So they'd gone on with their lives just as before, only dragging an infant along behind them. She'd grown up alone, really—aware even at a young age that her parents were more devoted to each other than they would ever be to her. The two of them were a world unto themselves, and she'd never been able to find a way into their inner circle—and once she was grown she'd stopped trying.

Now there was an occasional postcard for her from wherever they happened to be and infrequent phone calls made more from a sense of duty than any real need to stay in touch.

Annie hadn't been raised with a sense of tradition, and maybe that was part of the reason she'd so longed for a family of her own. So she could build traditions. Make for her daughter the kind of childhood she herself had always wanted.

So listening to John talk about his extended family was a little like trying to imagine life on Mars.

"Oh, yeah," he was saying, still patting Jordan's narrow back gently, "there's nothing the Parettis like more than a party. And the babies were passed around to whoever was handy. Including the kids."

"Really?" She had a mental image of a roomful

of adults standing around chatting while rows of children played hot potato with babies.

"Sure." He grinned when Jordan burped for him, then lowered her to the crook of his arm again and once more offered her the bottle. "An Italian child doesn't learn to walk until it's two or three. Their feet never hit the floor long enough to get the hang of it."

Annie laughed, only half-sure he was kidding.

"And what about that old phrase *woman's work?*" she asked.

"Never heard it," he said on a laugh. "At least, not in my house. My mom was a firm believer in her sons knowing how to cook and clean. She always said she didn't want our future wives coming to her with complaints."

Annie had the distinct impression she would really like John's mom.

"What about you?" he asked, his gaze settling on her. "What's your family like?"

"Small," she said, and folded her arms on the tabletop. "I'm an only child."

"Oh, man," he said wistfully, "how many times did I wish I could say *that* growing up?"

"You don't mean that," she said. She'd heard too much love in his voice when he'd described his family to believe that.

"Nah, I guess not. But at the time..." John

smiled for a moment at the memory. "When you're the youngest of three brothers, you end up being the punching bag—or the one who gets blamed for everything—or the one who gets left behind. But once we got older, it was kind of nice having them around." The baby fell asleep in his arms, and John took the bottle out of her mouth again and set it on the table.

He stared down at the tiny girl with an expression of such wonder that Annie's heart tightened in response. Why hadn't she found a man like him first? Why couldn't Mike Sinclair have been even *half* the man John Paretti was? Why hadn't she given her daughter a father worthy of her?

"What about your folks?" he asked, snatching her out of her woolgathering and drawing her back to the present. "What do they do?"

Safer ground, she told herself and gratefully snatched at the lifeline he'd inadvertently thrown her. "My father's an archaeologist," she said, "officially retired, but—you can take the archaeologist out of the dirt, but you can't take the dirt out of the archaeologist." She shrugged and smiled. "He's always off exploring—looking for new digs or for a dig he thinks has been handled badly."

He nodded, but didn't smile, almost as if he was hearing beyond her words to the sigh she hadn't uttered. "And your mom?"

"She's his assistant. They've been all over the world together. My father's even mentioned in a few college textbooks."

"And you went with them when you were a kid?"

"Yes," she said. "I'd visited Egypt, Israel and Iraq before I was six years old. We've been all over Europe and the Middle East."

"Sounds fascinating," he said quietly, thoughtfully. "We traveled a lot, too, what with my dad being in the Corps."

"Ah," she said, lifting one hand, "but did you have nannies who couldn't speak English?"

"No," he said softly, "I didn't. It sounds lonely."

"It was," she admitted, and realized that it was the first time she'd ever complained aloud about her unusual childhood. Sympathy and something else she didn't want to identify shone in his eyes as he looked at her, and Annie suddenly wanted a change of subject. Desperately. "I would have given anything for some older brothers to torment me," she said, a false note of humor coloring her voice.

Thankfully, he went along with her.

"That's easy for you to say," he told her, and gave her a smile that said he knew darn well what she was doing. "You weren't the one tied to a clothesline pole for a game of cowboys and Indians.''

"They didn't," she said.

"Like hell they didn't," John said, laughing now. "And as soon as they had their 'prisoner' tied up, they took off to play somewhere else without me tagging along. It was an hour before Mom found me."

"What happened to them?"

He grinned with obvious enjoyment. "Had their backsides smacked and sent to bed without dinner. *I*, on the other hand, had *cake*."

"Which you no doubt rubbed in their faces."

"Naturally."

"You know, I'm beginning to see how a little brother would be annoying."

He lifted one hand in mock exasperation and let it fall to the table. "No one understands me!" he proclaimed in a highly insulted tone.

Annie laughed, and John was glad he'd been able to chase the shadows from her eyes. Annie Foster was getting to him in a way that no one else before her had. Listening to her talk about a childhood spent with parents who pretty much ignored her presence made him want to call his own mom just to say thanks.

It also made him want to look out for Annie. To see that she never spent another lonely day.

And admitting to that, even if only silently, gave him a hard jolt.

"Oh, my God!" Lisa Jackson's voice came over the phone line so loudly that Annie jerked the receiver away from her ear. Unfortunately, not quickly enough. She winced as Lisa continued. "John delivered the baby? In a blizzard?"

"Actually," Annie said wryly, "we were in the cabin. The blizzard was outside."

"Cute, girlfriend. Real cute."

Annie looked across the room at John where he sat on the couch, holding the baby and talking to her as if she really understood him. Something soft and warm wrapped itself around her heart, and a melting sensation pooled in her knees. So she sat down.

"Is everything all right?"

"Everything's fine," she told her best friend, smiling. "Jordan's beautiful, and it finally stopped snowing. We may actually be able to drive down off the mountain by tomorrow or the next day."

If, she thought, the snowplow people were as efficient as the telephone company. They'd had the lines repaired almost as soon as the snow had stopped. And the minute the phone was working again, Lisa had called. She'd probably been dialing nonstop for the past couple of days.

"How are you getting along with John?" Lisa asked, and Annie's attention snapped back to the conversation.

Hmm…she had to answer that question carefully, since John could hear every word she said.

"Fine," she said, and knew that wasn't nearly what she wanted to say.

She'd like to tell Lisa that John Paretti was kind and tender and funny and sweet and strong. She wanted to say that he made her go weak in the knees. That her heartbeat staggered whenever he smiled at her. She wanted to tell her friend how Jordan responded to the man and how good he was with the baby.

But if she *did* say all of that out loud, it would make it real. So it was just as well, she thought, that she couldn't say any of it.

"Oh, yeah," Lisa said, "'fine' sounds like a good time."

John looked over at her and grinned. Annie's heartbeat thundered in her chest. *Fine* with one man could be better than *terrific* with another one.

"Fine's not bad," she said.

"Oh, God," Lisa muttered. "I can *hear* the sigh in your voice."

"No, you can't," she argued, though even she noticed she wasn't denying the fact that the sigh was there.

"Listen, honey, John's a great guy, but—"

"But?"

"It's just that you're not his type."

Well *that* stung. "Is that right?"

"Now, don't go getting all offended on me."

"Did I say I was?"

"No, but I heard it, anyway."

"Is there a problem?" John asked from across the room.

"No problem," Annie told him. "Lisa's just having a psychic moment."

"Great," he said, "ask her what we're having for dinner."

"Oh, ha-ha," Lisa said, obviously having heard John for herself. "Look, honey, you plus baby equals family. And that's not something John Paretti's looking for."

Not that she was interested or anything but, "And you know this how?"

"Peter and John are good friends, and Peter's always telling me about John's way with women...." She paused for a long moment and chuckled as she said, "I think Peter's living vicariously through John."

"Swell," Annie said, glancing at the man whose gorgeous face was highlighted by the flickering light and shadow cast by the dancing flames in the hearth.

A way with women, huh? Well, should she pause here to be surprised? Hardly. A man that good-looking, that...*male,* would hardly be living the life of a monk. Still, it hurt more than a little to think that his slow, easy smile was probably just a well-practiced routine. Which told her that, despite her best intentions, she'd already formed a sort of attachment to John. Perfectly natural, she told herself, while Lisa kept talking. After all, women falling in love with their doctor—or the man who delivered their babies—was practically a cliché.

"Are you okay, honey?" Lisa asked, and this time her voice, filled with concern, reached past Annie's preoccupation.

"Yeah," she said. "I'm great." Okay, not great, but she really didn't want to talk about this anymore. "And I'll call you when I get home, okay?"

"Sure, Annie. And you know, I'm sorry if I burst your bubble or something."

"You didn't," she said, determined to convince both herself and Lisa.

"If you're sure..."

"I am."

"Okay, then, I'll see you when you get home."

She said goodbye and hung up, letting her fingers trail along the back of the receiver.

"Bad news?" John asked.

Annie turned to look at him and couldn't stop

the nearly automatic tripping of her heart. Good Lord, she could be in some serious trouble here if she didn't get a grip on reality.

"No," she said firmly, and pushed herself to her feet. "Nothing's wrong. Lisa's just worried about me."

"Lisa's a born worrier."

"Yeah, she is. But she means well." Just as she'd meant well telling Annie to not start mooning over John Paretti. It wasn't her fault the warning had come too late.

John frowned slightly as he studied her, and she wondered what he was thinking even while she told herself it really didn't matter. She didn't need to understand him. Didn't need to know that he was a ladies' man. Didn't need to idly daydream or to speculate as to just what his kiss would be like.

These few days in the cabin were nothing more than stolen time. Snatched from the everyday world, they'd both been thrown into an unusual situation that would be ending all too soon.

When it ended, they'd go back to their own lives. And in reality, John Paretti would never look at her twice. Not that she would be looking, either. Of course not. She didn't need anyone else now.

She had Jordan.

And together the two of them were the only family they'd ever need.

Six

"**W**hat're you working on?" John came up behind her and looked over her shoulder.

Never taking her gaze from the screen, Annie said, "A new Web site for a prospective client."

Her fingers flew over the keys, and occasionally she tapped the mouse and colors streamed across the laptop screen. Then she'd mutter, chew at her bottom lip and start all over again. And he was becoming way too fond of watching her chew that lip of hers. In fact, he was dangerously close to offering to chew it *for* her.

Reining his hormones in, he told himself to get a grip and asked, "Why'd you delete that?" as he pulled a chair up and sank onto it. "It looked good." Not that he knew much about storks carrying babies, but it looked pretty good to him.

Now she did glance at him. "Good but not great." She sighed and added, "And I *need* great."

Night crouched outside at the window, but inside the cabin, warmth and light surrounded them. The baby was asleep in the next room, and Annie'd been ignoring him for too long. So, since she seemed determined to work, John had decided to help. Or at least bug her enough that she'd talk to him.

Pitiful, Paretti, he told himself. Simply pitiful. But, hey, could he help it if she was just so damned attractive? It's not as though he was *trying* to get turned on. It just sort of happened. Anytime she came into a room, God help him. He inhaled the pure, soft scent of soap and water and told himself he'd never again be able to take a shower without thinking of how that soap smelled on her skin. Oh, he was in deep trouble here and sinking too fast to yell for help.

If he'd wanted help...which he was pretty sure he didn't.

"What's so special about this client?" he asked, determined to keep his mind off showers and wet bodies and tangled limbs and—damn it.

"Oh, let's see." She tapped one finger against

her chin as if she was having to give that question some real thought. Then she looked at him. "Only that if I can land this account, it could *make* my business."

He glanced at the screen. "Tidy Didy Diaper Service? This is a make-or-break thing?"

"Hey," she told him, "it's a big company. If they hire me to update their site and maintain it for them, not only is it a personal and professional coup, the money will make my checkbook look *way* less pathetic."

Okay, now he felt guilty. Here he was thinking only of getting her into bed, and she was actually thinking of her future. He shouldn't be taking shots at what looked like a silly company, when it clearly meant everything to Annie. As a single mother, of course she'd be interested in doing whatever it took to grow her company and her bank account. Determination glittered in her eyes, and he thought he saw just a shadow of fear there, too. A fear that she wouldn't succeed. That she might let down the baby who was so dependent on her. And his insides twisted. She shouldn't be having to do this alone. That ex-boyfriend of hers should be doing his share, too. And like an idiot, he said so.

"Why don't you make Jordan's father pay child support at least?"

She went perfectly still. And after a long, slow

moment or two, she swiveled her head to look at him. Those deep-blue eyes of hers looked hard as marbles. "I don't want anything from him. I don't *need* anything from him."

"What about what Jordan needs?" he asked before he could think better of it.

She damn near flinched at the unspoken accusation, and an arrow of shame shot right through his heart. "I'm her mother. I'll give her what she needs."

"By working yourself to death for it?"

A short, sharp laugh shot from her throat. "To death? I'm sitting here in my robe at a kitchen table, tapping on some keys. For the first time in days, I might add."

Okay fine, so this was the first time he'd seen her actually working. But for God's sake. She just had a baby. "Yeah, well," he said pointedly, "you've been fairly busy."

"True. And now I'm working. So if you don't mind…" She turned around again and concentrated on the screen and the flickering logo of a weirdly dancing diaper she'd just created.

"You know…" he said as he watched the screen from over her shoulder.

"What?" Irritation colored that one word and a smarter man might have backed off. But he'd been raised in an Italian household, where shouting came as easily as hugging. A good fight or two never hurt anything.

"Maybe it would be better to have a dancing baby instead of a diaper?"

She slid him a glance. "He's not selling babies. He's selling diapers."

"True, but babies *wear* them."

"Yes, but—"

"That empty diaper just looks too weird. Like there's an invisible baby or something." He gave a mock shudder.

"I thought you were a Marine, not an advertising executive."

"Hey," he said, leaning his forearm on the back of her chair, "I'm a consumer."

"Of diapers?"

"It was just a suggestion." Why did she have to smell so damn good? Lifting one hand, he took a piece of her hair between his thumb and forefinger and rubbed it gently. It felt like silk, all clean and soft and shining. And he wondered what in the hell she'd say if she knew he was just enjoying the feel of her hair against his skin. At that thought, he moved his hand and sat back, deliberately keeping a bit more distance between them. Not enough distance, he told himself, but silently admitted that to feel safe right now, he'd have to be in California with her in Rhode Island, and that wasn't likely.

"A baby, huh?" she murmured, more to herself than to him.

"Why not?"

"Worth a try," she said and hit a few more keys. When nothing happened, she muttered an oath, hissed at the computer and slumped back in her chair, arms folded across her chest.

"Problem?"

"This stupid computer just isn't fast enough."

"Why use it then?" he asked as his gaze automatically went to the bottom lefthand corner of the screen's frame, searching for the computer's brand name. When he saw it, he winced.

"Because it's the best," she grumbled, and sat up to poke at a couple more keys.

"The best, huh? But not fast enough?"

"Nope." She tossed him a glance, then went back to the keyboard, her fingers flying like a concert pianist at Carnegie Hall. "Still, the P3 has better graphics, easier menus and a bigger memory than most of its class."

"Is that right?" John asked, smiling to himself.

"Oh, yeah," she said, tapping and clicking and humming to herself. "With a little more work and a bit more imagination, the P3 could take over the lion's share of the personal computer industry."

"Really?" Oh, he was enjoying this.

"It's a relatively small company right now," she

was saying. "Family held. What they need is to expand. Get some fresh blood in there."

"Younger blood, you mean."

"Not necessarily, though from what I hear, the old man who founded the company doesn't take kindly to change."

"How do you know so much about it?" he wondered aloud.

"I read the business section of the paper," she said. "Come on, sweetheart," she cooed to the computer, "one little baby, that's all I'm asking. Anyway," she went on talking as she worked, "apparently the old man wants his sons to take over, but they're not interested, and right now, he's trying to protect himself from a takeover. Though why his sons aren't interested is beyond me."

"Actually, that's the easy part," John told her. "None of us wants to leave the Corps for a desk job peddling computers."

Annie's fingers stopped dead on the keyboard, her right index finger poised over the letter *h*. "Us," he'd said. None of *us*. P3. Paretti Computer Corporation. John Paretti.

Oh, good God.

Slowly she turned around to look at him, hoping she was wrong. But one look into his pale-blue eyes, dancing with suppressed humor, told her she wasn't.

"You're one of *those* Parettis?" she asked unnecessarily.

"Yep. Surprise."

"I don't like surprises."

"Sorry about that."

He didn't *look* sorry. "You could have said something."

"I don't usually open up conversations by saying, 'I'm John Paretti, of the computer Paretti's.'"

"Okay, fine," she said, willing to give him that much. "But once I started complaining about the stupid thing, you could have said something."

"Why? I don't make 'em."

"Your father does."

"Don't I know it. And he's pretty much just how you described him, too. Hardheaded. Wants his own way. Doesn't like change. Wants his sons to come into the company and take it over. Fighting off bigger names who want to swallow the company."

"And this doesn't interest you?" Complete bafflement colored her tone. She heard it herself. But how could she help it? What kind of person didn't want to be involved in the family business? Especially *this* business?

He frowned slightly. "Not until recently."

"What changed?"

John pushed up from the chair, walked across the small kitchen floor to the counter and turned around, leaning his backside against it. Folding his arms across his chest, he looked at her, and Annie tried not to notice how well that green sweater fit him. Or just how long his legs looked, encased in those worn jeans of his. Heck, if he'd been wearing cowboy boots instead of tennis shoes, she might have climaxed just looking at him.

Whoops! Where had that come from?

Then he started talking, and she told herself to concentrate on his voice and his words.

"My dad's getting older. Although—" he paused and sighed "—I can't see him *ever* retiring. The point is, he needs us. Or at least one of us."

He didn't sound very happy about that at all. "And I'm guessing that you're considering throwing yourself on the sacrificial altar?"

He winced slightly and shook his head. "Okay, it might not be that bad, but still…"

"That bad?" Annie got up, too, and walked closer to him. Not *too* close, mind you. But close enough. "How can you not be interested in building that company? P3 is the best new computer to have come out in years."

"So Dad's always telling us," he said wryly.

"He's right," she said quickly.

"Excuse me," he told her, "weren't you just cussing at it a minute ago?"

She waved that aside. Everyone cursed at machinery. Technology was the devil. Still, it beat the heck out of chipping messages into a stone tablet with a hammer and drill. "Yes, but I didn't mean it. And your father built this company himself?"

"Yep," John said and let his head fall back. Staring at the ceiling, he went on. "Worked nights and weekends until he had it perfected. Then got a loan to start up the business, then left the Corps to run it. Now he wants *us* to leave the Corps to take over for him."

"And you don't want to."

"Hell, *none* of us wants to," John said. "This company isn't our dream. It's Dad's. We *like* being Marines."

"But it's your family business. How can you *not* want to be a part of it?"

He tilted his head to one side, studied her for a long moment, then asked, "And are you just busting to get into Daddy's archaeological digs?"

Direct hit. "No, but that's not really the same thing, is it?"

"Why?" he countered. "Because archaeology doesn't interest you."

"Exactly."

"Yeah, well," he told her flatly, "computers don't interest me."

"To each his own, I guess," she said, though she really couldn't understand why someone wouldn't want to be in on the ground floor of something as exciting as the computer industry. After all, the future was in technology, whether people liked it or not.

"That's what I always thought," John said, shifting his gaze until he was looking right at her. "But lately I've been thinking that one of us owes it to the old man to do what he wants."

"Meaning you," she said, instinctively knowing that John had already decided that he would be the brother to give up his dream for their father's sake.

He shrugged, but his eyes couldn't quite carry off the nonchalant attitude. There were shadows there. Deep, dark shadows, and she knew he wasn't at all pleased with the decision he was going to make. "Sam and Nick are married now. Starting families."

"Then wouldn't one of them make the more logical choice to leave the Marines and settle down?"

He laughed to himself at the notion of either one of his brothers as civilians. Not a chance. "No. They've already worked out the logistics of married life in the Corps. Their wives are with them on it.

No sense in disrupting lots of lives when I'm by myself.''

"Even if you're miserable?'' she asked, seeing the truth in his face, his eyes.

"Hell, misery doesn't last forever. Maybe once I figure out how to work the damn computer, it won't be so bad running the show.''

"Amazing,'' she said, thoughts whirling through her mind. Her own family couldn't be bothered to call and check on her. The last time she'd spoken to them, she'd been four months pregnant. Their disapproval of their unmarried, pregnant daughter had been palpable even on the phone lines, and they'd underlined that disapproval by not bothering to call her since.

Yet here John was, with a family that wanted him. Needed him. And he was doing everything he could to avoid being involved.

"I suppose you'd jump at the chance to run P3.''

"You bet,'' she said instantly. Then a moment later she asked, "I've always wondered. Why P3? How'd your father come up with that name?''

"*P* for Paretti and the *3* for his sons.''

"Ahh…''

He nodded. "Masters at guilt, we Italians. Even when he was starting out, I guess he figured that naming the computer after us would bring us all in on it.''

"And he was wrong."

"Up until now."

"So you've already made up your mind," she said, watching his face. "You're going to leave the Marine Corps."

"I haven't decided yet for sure, but yeah." His gaze shifted away from her, and he stared off into nothingness as if trying to imagine his life outside the Corps. "I just don't see any other way around it."

"I'm sorry," she said softly, watching his face as he slowly turned back to look at her.

He shrugged and gave her a smile that tugged at the edges of her heart, and Annie knew that this was a man who could easily shatter the best-laid defenses around a woman's soul.

"Hey," he said, "we do what we have to do. You'll work your butt off for Jordan."

"And you'll sign your life away out of duty to your parents."

"It's not like I'm going to be sent to the gulag," he told her on a short laugh. "The company's in Florida."

That's not how it looked from where she was standing, but she didn't have the right to say so, did she? They weren't lovers. Heck, they weren't even friends. Fate had thrown them together for a brief period of time, and that time was almost over.

He lifted one hand, reached out to briefly cup her cheek. The shock of warmth splintered throughout her body, and Annie damn near sizzled with it. When his hand dropped to his side again, she drew in a long, ragged breath. Good heavens, what was she doing here? Why was she allowing her hormones to turn her into a drooling pool of want?

She wasn't looking for a man.

She didn't *want* a man.

And maybe if she kept repeating that over and over again for the next ten years, her body might believe her.

Seven

"**Y**ou don't have to do this," Annie said for the third time in the past fifteen minutes.

"It's no problem," John told her. Head inside her car, busily strapping the new child seat into place, his voice came muffled, since he didn't bother to turn toward her.

"But you driving us home will leave your car here," she pointed out, beginning to feel just a bit like a broken record. She'd already told him all of this and it didn't seem to matter. He'd set his course and she had the distinct impression it would take a full battalion to make him change his mind.

The roads were clear, and Annie was anxious to

get home. Not so much because she missed her small, two-bedroom apartment. But because she really needed to get as far away as possible from a certain Marine. And his volunteering to drive her and the baby home wasn't going to make that easy.

"I'm perfectly fine," she said, meaning every word, despite the twinge of discomfort that resulted from any too-quick movements. But she was doing nicely. All she needed was a few more weeks to get back into shape—and a little distance from John Paretti to get her hormones back under control.

This time he did turn around. Those pale-blue eyes glittered and sent a shower of sparks dancing through her body. For heaven's sake.

Letting his gaze slide up and down her body in a slow, appreciative stare, he waited until he was looking directly into her eyes before saying, "I will admit you look good. Still, the baby's not even a week old. I don't want you driving down the mountain all alone. There may be spots in the road that haven't been cleared yet."

"And your car?" she asked, surrendering to the inevitable. John wasn't about to give in on this. She could see it in his eyes.

"I'll get Pete to drive me back up here to collect it." He climbed out of her car, waved one hand at the new car seat he'd gone into town that morning to buy and said, "There. We're all set."

All set. Now she had two car seats and one car. Ah, well, she couldn't very well drive all the way home with the baby cradled in her arms.

John reached out, laid one hand on her shoulder and squeezed gently. And blast if she didn't feel the imprint of each of his fingers—right through the fabric of her jacket, her shirt, her skin, all the way down to her bones. She wasn't quite sure what to do about it, either. It felt so...good to feel good again.

But the danger in that was all too clear to her. The last time she'd been led by her hormones and a heart that was too easily fooled, she'd been left alone and pregnant. Though she wouldn't trade Jordan for anything in the world, she also didn't want to make the same mistakes she had in the past. Oh, everyone made mistakes, she knew that. But at the very least she could make some new ones.

No, it didn't matter what she felt for John Paretti. And it didn't matter that he'd treated her with more tenderness, more gentleness than she'd ever experienced before. These feelings weren't real. None of them. They were based entirely on the unusual circumstance that had drawn John and her together in the first place. If he hadn't been here, if he hadn't delivered her baby, if they hadn't been so much like a...*family* in the last few days, none of this would be happening.

Family. The word shimmered in her mind like the pot of gold at the end of a rainbow. And for one brief moment she entertained the notion of how different her life might have been if only John had been her baby's father. A heartbeat later, though, she let that thought go. Pointless to wonder. To speculate. The simple truth was, John Paretti wasn't a part of her life. He was a part of a dream world that was now ending.

The best thing for her to do was get back to reality and put this little idyll where it belonged: in a dark corner of her mind and heart where dreams were kept once you woke up.

Her expression must have given her away because John bent his head and asked, "Hey, are you okay?"

"Sure," she said, much too quickly. He didn't believe her. His eyes told her that. But then why should he, when she didn't believe her, either? Still, she slipped out from beneath his hand and tried not to mourn the loss of his touch. "I'm fine," Annie said firmly, willing herself to be convincing. "Uh, why don't I just go in and finish packing so we can get going?"

Escaping, John thought. She might as well have had a neon sign hanging over her head flashing out the words, Back Off. So fine. He'd back off. For now. But damned if it was easy.

"Yeah," he said tightly, "go ahead." His gaze followed her as she scuttled for the house, and the sound of the closing door seemed overly loud in the still air.

Standing right beside her, he'd felt her withdraw. She was already pulling away from him. There was a sense of goodbye hanging in the air between them despite the fact that no one had actually said the word aloud.

His chest tightened as he turned around and leaned against the car. Folding his arms over his chest, he crossed his feet at the ankles and stared at the cabin with enough intensity he should have been able to see through the log walls to the woman beyond. She was ignoring him. Getting ready to treat this past week as if it were nothing more than a temporary blip on her radar screen. Hell, she hadn't even bothered to come up with a good lie. She hadn't had to finish packing. She'd packed everything the night before. She was ready to leave and had been for hours. Apparently, he told himself, she was way more eager for their time together to be over than he was.

And that fact didn't come easy. John had spent most of his adult life avoiding any woman who looked as though she might be the "happily ever after" kind. Not that he had anything against marriage. It just had never felt right for *him*.

Until recently, that is.

Which only gave him one more thing to think about.

How had one small woman, in the space of less than a week, slipped under his guard to wrap herself around his heart?

Maybe she was doing the right thing, here, he told himself. Maybe it would be best for both of them—all *three* of them—if he and Annie slipped back into their old lives and forgot about what had happened up here. But how could they? he wondered an instant later. There was Jordan. A beautiful, tiny scrap of a miracle, as living proof that they'd shared something amazing here. That they'd connected in a way few people ever did.

But it wasn't just about that, he admitted silently, despite the cold ripple of caution that slid along his spine. It was much more. Even his dreams had been affected. When he closed his eyes now, he saw *her* eyes. Her smile. He heard her voice, her laugh. He saw her clumsy attempts at diapering. He felt the closeness that had sprung up between them.

And he always woke up hungry.

For her.

Scowling to himself, he muttered a curse and pushed away from the car. Hell, he'd come up here hoping to come to a decision about his future. Instead he was more confused than ever. Only one thing was absolutely clear to him now: whether he remained a Marine or not, he wanted Annie in his life. Annie and her baby.

And it was painfully clear to him that she didn't feel the same way.

A week later John stood on base, squinting into the morning sun and letting his gaze slide across the assembled MPs waiting for his orders. His mind wandered as he stared at those impassive faces, and he found himself not thinking about the current problem, but about Annie. He wondered what she was doing.

If she was all right.

If she missed him as much as he did her.

God, he'd never lived through such a long week.

"Gunnery Sergeant Paretti?"

John blinked, looked to his left and saw Peter staring at him as if his head was on fire. "What?"

Peter flicked his gaze toward the still-waiting men, then gave a half shrug. Lowering his voice, he reminded, "You wanted to tell the men about—"

"Yeah!" John said, shaking his head in a futile attempt to dislodge thoughts of Annie and the baby. Good thing he wasn't working with hand grenades today. "All right, listen up," he said, his voice naturally falling into the everyday roar he reserved for shouting to the troops. "Colonel Castellana called."

Someone in the back groaned.

"Shut up back there," John shouted, then continued. "She's at it again. She's got the Colonel's car, and he wants her stopped before she reaches the main gate."

"Can we shoot her?" someone else asked.

One corner of his mouth twitched, but John didn't let the smile take hold. Hell, he couldn't blame the big mouth for asking. The Colonel's oldest daughter was a trial. At sixteen, she had long red hair, big green eyes, a wild streak and a smile that could drop a man at fifty paces. She was forever snatching her father's prized T-bird and taking it for a high-speed spin around base. Then it was left to the MPs to catch her, corner her and escort her back home.

Teenage girls. It was enough to make a man seriously consider a vasectomy.

But back to the subject at hand. "Only if she shoots first," he said, then let his gaze shift across the young faces watching him. Hell, were corporals getting younger every year? Most of this bunch looked as though they should be playing football on a high school field.

A car horn beeped, and every man assembled turned his head to the right in time to see Amy

Castellana, in her daddy's T-bird, lift one hand in a wave as she sped past, red hair flying like a bull-fighter's cape.

"There she goes," John yelled. "Catch her!"

Ten men scrambled for their cars, and in seconds John and Peter were left standing in a cloud of dust kicked up by dozens of spinning tires.

"That girl's going to cost her father his next star if she isn't careful."

John stared off after the convoy of white sedans chasing the T-bird and half chuckled to himself. "If the Colonel was interested in being a General, he'd find a way to lock her down." He half turned to look at his friend. "I think he *enjoys* the girl's spirit."

"Yeah, you're probably right." Peter shook his head. "Still, makes me want to rethink the whole 'having a kid' thing."

"At least they're not born teenagers," John said, remembering Jordan's sweet face and tiny hands. How much had she changed? he wondered. A week was a long time to a baby.

"You've got that look in your eye again."

Yanked out of his thoughts, John shot Pete a quick glare and muttered, "What look?"

"The look you've had ever since you came back from the mountain."

Okay, he wasn't going there. Not with Pete. Not now. "You're nuts."

He turned and headed back toward his office, and Pete was just a step or two behind him.

"I'm nuts, huh?" he said. "Then how come when you walk around base these last few days, you're noticing all the babies in strollers?"

John scowled to himself. "It's my job to make sure people are safe on base."

"Uh-huh."

He stopped dead, whirled around and gave Peter a glare that should have fried him. His friend didn't look impressed. "Butt out, Pete. Leave it alone."

"Wish I could."

"Why the hell can't you?"

"Because Lisa's driving me crazy."

"About what?" he shouted, throwing both hands high.

"She wants to know what went on between you two when you were at the cabin."

John sighed, then reached up to tug the brim of his cover down lower over his eyes. "She knows what happened. I delivered Annie's baby."

"She says there's more."

"She's wrong." Of course, she wasn't. But he couldn't admit to that. He wasn't about to give Lisa any more ammunition for speculation until he'd had time to start working on Annie. The plan had been to give her a couple of weeks to settle in with the baby. To miss him. But the plan was about to change. Mainly because *he* was missing *her*.

"I don't know what's going on, and maybe it's none of my business." Peter gave him a long, level look. "But Annie's a friend, John. And she's had a rough time."

All right, this he understood. Lisa's intuition and Annie's wariness left him perplexed. Peter's concern was something else, though. But it went against the grain that someone besides *him* was protecting Annie. Worse yet was that his friend wanted to protect Annie *from* John.

"I know," he said, trying to remember that Pete was only trying to look out for someone he cared about. "And I'm not interested in giving her any more grief."

"What are you interested in exactly?" Pete asked, studying him.

"That's between me and Annie," John said tightly.

And silently he told himself it was high time he threw his "plan" out the window and convinced Annie that he was the man for her.

"She won't stop crying," Annie said, clutching the phone in an iron grip.

"Maybe she's hungry?" Lisa's voice sounded as hesitant as Annie felt.

Oh, this just wasn't going well at all. She'd wanted to be a perfect mother, and she couldn't even figure out how to stop her baby from crying.

It had all seemed so easy that first week in the cabin with John. He'd helped in a quiet, unassuming way, and she'd hardly noticed her own shortcomings. But now that she was on her own, she had to face the facts. She just wasn't cut out for this, she told herself. As much as she loved Jordan, she was just a lousy mommy.

And her baby deserved better.

"She's not hungry," she all but whined into the receiver as her gaze locked on the screaming infant lying in her little jumpy cradle. "She just ate a half hour ago."

"Gas?" Lisa asked.

"I don't know," Annie said, and reached out with one hand to stroke Jordan's tummy. The baby squirmed against her touch as if she sensed that Mommy was lost and there wouldn't be any help coming from that quarter.

"Well, maybe she just wants to cry," her friend suggested.

The blind leading the blind, Annie thought grimly. Lisa knew even less about children than she did. And for the first time in years Annie wished that she had normal parents. People she could turn to for answers. For comfort. For *help,* for Pete's sake.

Tucking the receiver between her ear and her shoulder, she picked Jordan up and cuddled her close. Maybe she'd get lucky, she thought. Maybe she'd stumble onto the answer to Jordan's distress.

Panic bubbled in her chest.

The baby's screams tore at her heart.

Tears burned her eyes.

And the doorbell rang.

"I've gotta go," Annie said, her throat closing around the knot of tears lodged there. "Someone's at the door."

"Do you want me to come over?" Lisa asked.

Desperately, Annie thought, but didn't say. *She* was the mommy here. It was up to her to find her way through the minefield of parenthood. And she'd do it. For Jordan. Her sweet baby was well worth the effort this was going to cost her.

"No," she said before she could change her mind and beg her friend to rush to her aid. "I can do this."

"I know you can."

The doorbell rang again.

"Gotta go," Annie said, already turning to hang up the phone.

"Call me later."

"Okay, bye."

She hung up the phone and, still jiggling the crying baby in her arms, walked across the room. Probably her neighbor, she thought, coming to complain about the noise. But it wasn't her neighbor.

It was the cavalry.

Eight

"Oh, thank God!" She'd never been so happy to see anyone in her whole life. "Come in, come in."

"That's some welcome," John said with a grin, and stepped into the apartment the moment Annie moved back out of his way.

"You have no idea," she said over the baby's screeching. She looked up into those familiar blue eyes and a wave of relief swamped her. It was as if she'd been drowning, going down for the third time, and someone had just tossed her a lifeline.

An extremely gorgeous, totally desirable lifeline.

"Miss me?" he asked, and the deep rumble of his voice carried easily over Jordan's cries.

Oh, yeah. Annie had missed him. More than she had wanted to admit. But she'd told herself that it was only natural. After all, they'd spent five or six straight days and nights together. They'd lived out of each other's pockets in that small cabin. He'd become a part of her routine. An important cog in her well-oiled machine. Plus, he'd seen her safely through labor and childbirth. That alone was bound to create a strong connection.

But even she didn't believe all of that. Sure, she'd become used to him. But, heck, you could become used to something annoying, too. That didn't mean you'd miss it when it was gone.

Nope. There was way more going on here than a simple disruption of a routine. She could lie to herself all she wanted, but even Annie had to recognize the rush of pleasure dancing through her at the moment for what it was.

Excitement at seeing him again.

This couldn't be a good thing.

"I missed you, too," he said, and reached out to touch her cheek. A splinter of heat shot through her at the too-brief contact and she told herself she was going to have to get a grip on those obviously still rampaging hormones.

"Hello, sweetheart," John was saying, and Annie's jaw dropped—until she realized he was speaking to the baby. The small flutter of delight that had momentarily rippled through her quickly died away, and she intended to pretend it had never been there in the first place. After all, she didn't want him calling her ''sweetheart'' anyway, right?

He scooped Jordan up into his arms and smiled into her scrunched-up, beet-red face. Her little legs curled up toward her body, and her spine stiffened as she let loose with another howl loud enough to shatter glass.

Her mother winced. ''She's been crying for hours,'' Annie whispered, and wondered if he heard the whine in her voice as clearly as she did.

''It's good exercise,'' he said, shooting her a quick smile before looking back at the baby. ''Strengthens her lungs, lets her kick her legs and wave her arms.''

''Oh,'' Annie said, pitching her voice to carry over the din, ''I think her lungs are plenty strong.''

He grinned and lowered the baby until she was lying belly down along the length of his forearm, her head cradled in one wide palm. Then he stepped into the ''sway and soothe'' rhythm that Annie had already tried—and failed at—several times.

Naturally, Jordan quieted right down for him.

And Annie was so pathetically, everlastingly grateful, she didn't even resent his obvious way with the baby.

Silence. Blessed silence.

The lack of sound almost hurt her still-ringing ears.

"Man," John said, unknowingly shattering the glorious peace with a question, "just what kind of bomb was it that got set off in here?"

Annie followed his gaze as he looked around the small living room of her two-bedroom apartment. She heard herself sigh and realized anew just how out of orbit her life really was.

Before Jordan's birth the apartment had been ruthlessly neat. A place for everything and everything in its place. Annie's natural instinct for order had shown in everything from the alphabetized spices in her cupboard to the fact that she didn't even *have* a junk drawer. Now, though, her whole apartment was a junk drawer.

Baby things lay scattered across the furniture and the rug. Toys, bottles, diapers, clothes, shoes, practically everything Jordan owned was on display. There was a swing in the corner near Annie's china cabinet and a floor mobile on a quilt spread on the floor. Stuffed animals perched on the couch and chairs as if they were guests waiting for lunch to be served.

Dishes were stacked in the kitchen sink and she didn't even care, she thought with an inward sigh. She was just so darned tired. She felt as though she hadn't slept in years. Why had no one told her just how hard the mommy life really was?

But she knew the answer to that one. If word got out about the difficulties of caring for babies, it would bring the population explosion to a grinding halt. And the economy couldn't take that. Toy stores. Clothing manufacturers. Obstetricians. They were all in on the conspiracy.

Oh, boy, she thought, lifting one hand to push her hair up and off her forehead, she was more tired than she thought.

"Hell, Annie," John said, tipping her chin up with the tips of his fingers, "you don't look much better than the apartment."

"Gee, thanks."

He smiled, and that half dimple winked at her from his cheek. Oh, good God.

"I just meant you look a little tired."

"No," she said, and walked over to the couch. "I'm a *lot* tired." Sinking down into the over-stuffed cushions, she sighed and felt her body melt. Maybe sitting hadn't been such a good idea. As long as she was standing, moving around, she could cope. Once she sat down, though, it was all over.

"You're running your mom ragged aren't you, sweet stuff?" John murmured as he idly stroked the baby's back.

"Who knew it would be this hard?" Annie asked aloud, not really expecting an answer.

"It's not hard," he told her as he came closer, "it just takes practice."

"Practice, huh?" she asked, drawing her feet up and curling her legs beneath her. "If you suck at something, all the practice in the world isn't going to help. You'll just suck slightly less."

He laughed, and she mustered the energy to lift her head and glare at him. "It's not funny."

"Sure it is," he said, easing down onto the arm of the sofa beside her. "You're being too hard on yourself, Annie."

"Yeah, right." She shook her head, looked at her now-blissfully sleeping daughter and said, "Look at this place, John. Heck, look at *me!*" Ruffling her hair with one hand, she used the other to wave at her rumpled, baby food stained clothing. "I'm a wreck."

He smiled again, but she paid no attention.

"I'm a college graduate," she muttered, more to herself than to him. "Did you know I have a masters in computer science?"

"No," he said quietly, "I didn't."

"Well, I do. And I minored in child psychology!" She threw her hands up and let them fall back into her lap. "I wanted to be able to understand my kids. To be a good... good—" her voice cracked, she gulped in a breath and finished lamely "—*mother.*"

Shifting the baby slightly, John reached over to stroke Annie's hair back from her face. Helplessness filled him and he didn't much care for the feeling. Hell, he'd thought he was doing her a favor by quieting the baby. But now, looking at the big, silent tears coursing down Annie's face, he thought maybe he'd made a mistake.

Somehow, just by being here, by getting Jordan settled down, he'd made Annie feel even worse. Damn it.

"You *are* a good mother," he said, willing her to believe him.

She shook her head, unfolded her legs and wrapped her arms around them, drawing her knees up close to her chest. "No. I'm not. And even Jordan knows it, poor baby."

"Come on," he said, shifting the baby again and, when she stirred, instinctively jiggling her gently. "You don't have to be the best at everything right off the starting line."

Annie lifted her head to look up at him. "Yes, I do," she said. "I'm all she's got. She's depending on me to do this right. To give her the kind of life she deserves."

"And you will," he said, even though somewhere inside him the words *we will* echoed softly.

Surprised, he waited to feel the flash of sheer mortal terror most men experienced when even a stray thought of marriage and forever entered his mind. It didn't come.

She laughed shortly, but there was no humor in it, and John winced at the sound.

"How?" she asked. "I can't even make her stop crying."

"Babies cry," he told her gently. "That's just part of the package."

"I know that, it's just—"

"Just what?" his voice was soft, low, intimate, and he hoped she didn't hear the need in it.

"What if I never get it?" she asked, worry coloring her tone. "What if I never learn how to be a good mom?"

A sheen of tears made her eyes glitter at him in the afternoon sun streaming in through the front window. Her brow was furrowed and her lips were clamped tightly together in an effort to stop their trembling.

His heart twisted in his chest. She looked so fragile. So beaten. So tired. All the spirit he'd seen in her at the cabin was gone. And that tore at him. He shouldn't have stayed away this week. He should have gone with his gut and pressed his case right away.

But *should haves* didn't mean a thing. This was now. And first things first.

"You *are* a good mother," he said, staring deeply into her eyes.

She shook her head, but before she could speak, he continued.

"You love her, Annie. That's all any baby ever really needs."

She took a breath, held it, then released it slowly as her gaze shifted to the tiny baby he held cradled on one arm. "I *do* love her," she murmured, stroking her fingertips along her daughter's cheek. "More than I ever thought it possible to love anyone."

He caught her hand with his and gave it a squeeze. "Then stop sweating the small stuff," he said. "Hell, crying's the easy part. Just wait till she's arguing with you about her curfew!"

She laughed, just as he'd hoped she would. "No arguments," she said solemnly. "She's not dating until she's twenty-five."

He looked down into the baby's innocent face and thought, nope. *Thirty* had a nice ring to it.

Then she folded her fingers around his and held on tight. "I'm so glad you came over today, John."

"So am I, Annie," he said, his gaze shifting to move over her features with a slow, loving caress, "so am I."

Seconds ticked past, and John's gaze dropped to her mouth. Hunger clawed at him. Good old-fashioned *need* reared its ugly head, and he nearly choked on the rush of desire. Being here with her was almost enough to bring him to his knees, even knowing that nothing could happen between them. Not yet. Hell, not for another few weeks, at least. But damned if it wouldn't be worth the wait. Two weeks he'd known this woman and one solid week of it they'd been apart and it didn't seem to matter.

He wanted her more than anything or anyone else in the world.

And he'd do whatever he had to do to convince her that she needed him, too.

Once, he thought as he noticed her eyelids drooping, she was conscious enough to appreciate his charms.

She sucked in a gulp of air and slowly drew her hand free of his. Then she smiled nervously, lifted both hands and rubbed her eyes. "I'm sorry about getting all teary on you."

"No problem." Hell, she could cry on his shoulder for the rest of her life.

"I just feel like I haven't slept in—"

"Days?" he asked.

"Years." She shot her daughter a quick, loving look. "Jordan seems to have a fondness for late-night chats and way-too-brief naps."

This he could take care of, he thought. "I remember my cousin Tina," John said and stood up slowly, carrying the baby toward the portable crib set up against the far wall. "When her son Jack was born? She swore she didn't sleep for the first two weeks. But she had her husband to do backup."

"Yeah well…"

He laid Jordan down and covered her with a lightweight blanket. Then, standing up, he turned around to face her and said, "So, why don't you let me be your backup today?"

She blinked, stifled a yawn and asked, "What?"

John crossed the room to her side, pulled her to her feet and said, "Go to bed."

"I can't," she argued, glancing from John to the baby and back again. "The apartment's a wreck and now that Jordan's asleep, I should—"

"Get some sleep?"

"I wish I could," she admitted, but then slid a glance at her laptop, sitting open on the cluttered kitchen table. "But even if I don't clean, I should finish that Web site design…"

"The dancing baby?"

"That's the one."

"Do it tomorrow."

"It's due tomorrow afternoon."

"Do it in the morning."

She yawned again and shook her head reluctantly. "No time. Jordan—"

"Annie," he said, laying both hands on her shoulders and waiting until she looked up at him to continue. "Go to sleep. I'll look after Jordan. You can't work if you're in a coma."

"Yeah, but—"

"No buts," he said, turning her toward the hallway and the bedrooms beyond. The door on his left was open, and one peek told him this was Jordan's room. A mural of cartoon teddy bears and tigers and bunnies danced along the wall, and over the crib hung a mobile of stars and moons in bright, primary colors.

Not a good mother, he thought. Right. She'd made sure Jordan had whatever she needed and the rest would come. If Annie'd give herself half a chance.

"I don't know, John," she was saying even as she opened the door to her bedroom and stepped inside.

The curtains were closed and the small, elegantly furnished room looked dark and cozy. Perfect for an afternoon nap. A green-and-white quilt lay across a queen-size bed, and a mountain of pillows were piled against the headboard. There was nothing John wanted more than to lie down on the bed with her, but right now his protective instinct was even stronger than the urge to touch her, hold her, kiss her…okay, better derail *that* particular train of thought.

Leading her across the hardwood floor, he sat her down on the edge of the bed, then bent down to untie her sneakers and slip them off.

"John," she said, her voice already clouded with the promise of sleep, "you don't have to do this. I'm not helpless."

"I know that," he said, standing up and easing her down onto the mattress. "But it makes me feel good, taking care of you. So don't bruise my fragile ego by refusing, okay?"

A quick half smile dusted across her face as she snuggled down into the nest of pillows. She sighed, stretched and closed her eyes. "Well, since you put it that way…"

He grinned at her and reached for the crocheted afghan folded neatly at the foot of her bed. Opening it up, he flicked it into the air and let it fall gently down on top of her. Then he tugged the edge of the blanket up to her chin. For himself he paused long enough to smooth her hair back from her forehead, then bent low to drop a kiss at her hairline.

"God, I missed you," he whispered, wanting her to know that she hadn't been far from his thoughts. He straightened up, looked down at her and opened his mouth to tell her more, then caught himself and snapped his mouth shut again.

She was asleep.

The steady rise and fall of her chest, the deep rhythm of her breathing in the quiet room told him she'd been more tired than either of them had thought. As he watched her, she rolled onto her side and curled up, one hand reaching across the pillows to the emptiness beside her.

Alone, he thought. She'd been alone too long, and whether she knew it yet or not, she'd already taken the first step toward him. She was trusting him with Jordan. The most important person in the world to her.

Now all he had to do was get her to trust him with her heart.

Annie awoke to complete darkness.

And she didn't even remember going to bed.

A split second later memory kicked in.

"Jordan!" She threw the afghan to one side, leaped out of bed and raced for the door. Her baby. How could she have slept so long? What if Jordan needed her? What if John hadn't been as capable as he'd thought? What if...?

She flung open the door, charged down the short hall, burst into the living room and skidded to a stop. The room was clean. Toys, clothes, baby paraphernalia all stashed away, the room looked the way it used to, back when Annie still had time to care about such things. And unbelievably enough, there was the scent of spaghetti sauce drifting in the air.

But she really wasn't paying much attention to those things. Instead, she focused on John Paretti—professional soldier—sitting on the couch, in her now-tidy living room, Jordan lying peacefully in the crook of his arm. He held a baby bottle, and while Jordan slurped happily at her meal, he talked to her. Smiled at her.

And Annie felt her heart melt.

Nine

"**I** found formula in the fridge, so when she started fussing, I just fed her," John said as he looked up and met her gaze. "Hope that's all right."

"Sure," she said, not bothering to explain that she'd stopped nursing because her doctor had told her she wasn't producing enough milk for the baby. Another small failure, she thought wryly. But at least Jordan was thriving, and the upside was, when help was available she could take advantage of it. If she was still nursing, John wouldn't have been able to feed the baby. "But you shouldn't have let me sleep so long."

He shrugged. "You needed it."

Had she ever. She felt better than she had in days. Rested, alert and, now that she was completely conscious, aware of a certain look in Gunnery Sergeant Paretti's pale-blue eyes.

Annie's stomach pitched, and a slow, deep throbbing pulsed to life inside her. She knew that feeling. Heck, she remembered it. Vaguely. It was the same feeling that had brought her here, to this point in her life. Except there was one major difference: this flash of desire that John Paretti kindled in her was far stronger than anything she'd ever known before. And he didn't even have to touch her to stoke the flames licking at her insides. A single look was enough to rocket her heartbeat and send warmth shooting to her center. Oh, this couldn't be good, she thought as her knees liquefied, and she locked them to keep herself from sliding onto the floor.

How in heaven did the man manage to look so damn sexy while cradling a baby?

"I made dinner," he said.

Oh, God. He *cooked*, too.

"And I thought after we eat, we could play with that Web site that's got you so worried."

He gave her a slow smile, and Annie heard her goose being cooked. Not only did he let her sleep, he'd cleaned her apartment, made dinner, cared for her baby and was now offering to help her in her work.

The man was a saint.

With just enough devil in his eyes to be completely devastating.

Oh, man, she was in some serious trouble. And the worst part of it was, she was loving it.

Once the dishes were done and the baby was asleep and Annie had taken a shower, John sat beside her at the kitchen table and watched as she created an amazing little piece of computerized art.

The dancing baby shuffled across the screen, stepping on a set of building blocks. Each block held the key for a different page, and as the baby's feet touched one, it lit up and played a tune. Each block had its own special song that sent the baby into a series of different dance moves. Dazzling color splashed in the background, and the printing font she'd chosen was easy to read and had the feel of a child's first printing attempt.

It was damned clever.

"You're really good at this, you know?" he said, and was rewarded when she turned to him and grinned.

"Thanks," she said, "but the dancing baby was your idea, remember?"

Of course he remembered. He remembered everything about that week in the mountains. "Yeah, but having an idea and making it work are two different things." He leaned in closer, close enough to inhale the scent of soap and shampoo and Annie.

He dragged that scent deep within him, even knowing that it would only fuel the dreams of her that came nightly.

"And," she said, "to be fair, it was your idea to use kids blocks as the page keys."

"True, but you're the one who added the different music and made the baby a miniature Fred Astaire."

"Ah," she said, sending him another quick smile. "A mutual admiration society."

"You have no idea," he murmured. Admiration didn't even come close to describing what he felt for her. There was so much about her that appealed to him. Her strength, her vulnerability, her warm smile and loving touch. Her talent and her quick mind. The way she looked at Jordan and her determination to be everything her child needed. Hell, he even liked how she'd organized her boxes of cereal by height.

But mostly he loved how she made him feel just by being around her. John gave in to his need to be closer to her and reached over to touch one of the soft blond curls dangling just behind her ear.

His fingertips brushed against her skin, and she jumped slightly but didn't pull away. Progress, he thought and indulged himself by enjoying the feel of her silky hair between his fingers. God, he wanted to touch her so badly his palms itched.

"John," she said, her voice hushed, strained with what he hoped was the same desire rushing through him.

"You look beautiful in computer screen light," he said, making her chuckle. "And I need to kiss you more than I need my next breath."

Her laughter stopped dead. She swiveled her head to look at him. He read the flash of hunger in her eyes. And in an instant his own need quickened, blossomed until it nearly strangled him.

She sucked in a long, shaky breath, then said, "I don't think—"

"Good," he said, pulling her to her feet. "Don't think. Now's not the time for thinking, Annie." She tipped her head back to stare up at him. "Now's the time for tasting," he said, bending closer to her, "touching," closer still, "needing."

And his mouth came down on hers. At the first touch of her lips, John felt his control crumble. He wanted her desperately and needed her even more. Drawing her into the circle of his arms, he pressed her tightly to him, knowing she could never be close enough. She lifted her arms, wrapping them around his neck, and then she tilted her head, meeting his kiss with an urgency all her own.

On a sigh her lips parted beneath his, and John

seized the moment. His tongue swept into her warmth, exploring, tasting. She returned his caress, and their tongues clashed in a wild, warm dance that left them both struggling for air and still it wasn't enough.

One hand on her behind, he pulled her hips close, letting her feel exactly what she did to him, letting her know that he was hard and ready and eager for her. She gasped and arched into him, pressing her own body against his strength, and he damn near lost it.

Tearing his mouth from hers, he worked his way along her jaw and down the length of her throat. He paused at the base, to taste the thundering beat of her pulse, enjoying the fact that its crashing rhythm matched his own.

She sighed again, and that soft sound propelled him onward. Her hands clutched at his back, his shoulders. He felt her hands moving along his spine and wanted nothing more than to tear his shirt off so that nothing would stand between them. Instead he lavished more attention on her. He trailed damp, hot kisses across her chest and cursed softly when he met the edge of her scoop-necked blouse. He wanted more. Needed more. And at her growl of frustration, he realized *she* needed it, too.

Walking her backward, he braced her against the kitchen counter, then went down onto his knees in front of her. Lifting the hem of her shirt, he slid his hands up, up, until he captured her small, firm breasts in his palms. Then, while she sagged against the counter, he rubbed her nipples between his fingers until they peaked, and she was shivering.

"John," she whispered and he looked up at her. "I can't...*we* can't...it's too soon after the baby and..."

"Shh..." he said with a shake of his head. "I know. I know, I just need to touch you. Let me touch you, Annie. Let me feel my way around you."

He tweaked her nipples and she let her head fall back as she groaned tightly and curled her fingers around the edge of the counter. "Yes, John. Yes."

That's all he needed to hear. He leaned into her, kissing her breasts, one after the other, letting his tongue and teeth drive her to the brink of madness. And when she was barely holding on, he shifted, kissing her rib cage, her stomach, her abdomen. And then he reached for the waistband of her shorts and slowly pulled them and the scrap of lace-edged panties down and off her shapely legs.

"John?"

His hands smoothed over her skin, and when she trembled in his grasp, he steadied her.

"John," she said again, her voice breathy, strained, "maybe we should stop this now."

"Not quite yet," he murmured as he leaned in toward her and covered her with his mouth.

"Oh, my!" Annie said, and slapped her hands more firmly on the counter's edge. "You shouldn't be—we shouldn't be—oh my…"

He worked her most-sensitive flesh with his tongue and his lips. He took her on a wild ride that had her gasping his name and spreading her legs for him eagerly. She shifted clumsily against the counter, trying to give him more room, trying to draw him closer.

He touched her gently, dipping one finger into her warmth while at the same time, licking at her center as though her body held an exquisite dessert.

She moved one hand to the back of his head, holding him in place, silently demanding that he finish what he'd started. That he take her to the edge and beyond. That he give her what they both wanted so desperately.

And John relished it all. He loved that she was so liquid and warm in his arms. That she wanted him as much as he did her. That he was able to give her this—until he was able to give them both so much more. He tasted her, licked at her and touched her until she was writhing against him. And it wasn't enough. He wanted to push her higher and faster than she'd ever gone before. He wanted to be the man who took her places she hadn't dreamed existed.

Annie held on tightly, knowing that if she let go of him—or the counter—she might very well slide off the edge of the world. His mouth. His lips. Dear heaven, his tongue. Her body felt as if it was on fire from the inside. Her hips rocked into him, she went up on her toes as if trying to reach the peak he was driving her toward.

And yet there was a small, hidden part of her that never wanted to reach that peak. She wanted this to go on and on. To never end. She wanted him with her, on her, in her, as she'd never wanted anything else in her life. She'd been touched before. She'd had sex. Knew the brief, tingle of pleasure that accompanied it. But she'd never known feelings like this.

So strong.

So overwhelming.

She looked down and watched John take her. Watched him stake a claim on her body, on her heart. And while she watched, that tiny tingle of pleasure erupted, leaving her, as always, pleased, but somehow incomplete. At least in this case, the build to that tiny tingle had been more enjoyable.

Then her body stirred and she realized with a start that it wasn't over. Annie's breath caught as the tingle grew and spread, sending tentacles of warmth and spirals of surprise spinning throughout her body. She'd never experienced anything like this. Didn't know what to do. Couldn't breathe. This wasn't right, was it? Shouldn't it be over now, with John easing back with a satisfied smile on his face?

She shifted, uncomfortable now as the tingling became electrified. As John's mouth took her further than she'd expected. Further than she'd known she could go. Her hips rocked wildly and her breath staggered in and out of her lungs. She clutched him to her as an unexpected wave of sensation crashed down on top of her, dragging her down, down, and then pushing her up higher than she'd ever gone before. She called out his name when her soul exploded and moaned as the pulsing throbs slowly ebbed, leaving her a limp rag completely at John Paretti's mercy.

He stood up, pulling her close, wrapping his arms around her and holding her up while she sagged into him.

When her heart stopped trying to fly out of her chest, she tipped her head back, smiled up at him and said, ''And you *cook,* too.''

''Ooh-rah,'' John muttered, and kissed the top of her head.

Amazing, she thought as she let him lead her into the living room and onto the couch. He cradled her against his chest, and Annie didn't even seem to notice that all she was wearing was her shirt.

His hands moved over her skin, and it felt so good, so right that she nestled closer against him. "That was…"

"Good?" he prodded.

She laughed shortly. "Oh, way better than good," she assured him, then looked up at him. "But what about you? I mean…" she said in a rush, "it doesn't seem fair that you're…well… really you're *not*—"

He kissed her, long and slow and hard, then lifted his head and looked directly into her eyes. "I'm good," he said tightly, and she heard the strain in his voice so she didn't quite believe him. "Don't get me wrong," he continued, "I want you so bad, my teeth hurt with it."

A flush of pure female pride stole over her.

"And as soon as you're able, I'm going to show you a few more tricks."

Her stomach skittered, and her mouth went dry. "Is that a threat?" she asked.

"It's a promise."

Oh, boy.

Three weeks passed so quickly Annie felt as though she was caught inside a whirlwind. She'd never really paid much attention to the passing of time before. But now, looking into her daughter's tiny face, she noticed. Every day brought a new change. Every morning found Jordan a little more aware of her surroundings, a little more willing to smile and play. A little more forgiving of her still not-so-hot mommy.

But in her own defense, she had improved quite a bit. Diapers no longer slid off Jordan's bottom, Annie was able now to recognize the difference between an "I'm hungry" cry and an "I'm bored" cry, and she was no longer terrified that she would somehow emotionally scar her daughter if she did make an occasional mistake.

And she had to admit that a lot of her newfound confidence was due to John. He made it all seem so easy. So natural. It was hard to be worried about making a mistake when John was there to laugh with her over them. They'd even managed to set a routine of sorts, which comforted the organizational side of Annie's nature. And John had become a big part of that routine, which delighted the completely irrational side of her nature.

John Paretti had somehow slipped into her life, her mind and her heart without her even realizing it. She hardly remembered a time when he wasn't a part of her everyday world.

He was at the apartment three or four times a week, and though a small voice inside her kept warning her not to let him get so close, she wasn't listening.

Jordan's face lit up whenever he came into a room, and Annie had the distinct feeling hers did, too. Just hearing his step on the walk or his voice from the next room was enough to spur her heart into a wild gallop.

And the fact that his kisses set fire to her soul and his hands were absolutely magical wasn't exactly helping.

But it was so much more than physical want, and that was the really terrifying part. He was fun. He made her laugh. He loved Jordan. And she felt safe with him.

Which probably wasn't a good thing at all.

It wasn't so long ago that she'd thought Mike Sinclair was the be-all and end-all of her dreams. She'd felt safe then, too. She'd felt loved. Wanted. And then he'd left her so fast her head spun for a week. She'd survived Mike leaving.

But she wasn't at all sure she would survive if she actually counted on John and he walked away. That wouldn't happen, though. She wouldn't allow herself to care that much. She would just enjoy his company while she had it and not think about the future. A future that, without John, looked mighty empty, she thought.

"Oh, for heaven's sake," Annie muttered, "now

is not the time.'' She finished packing up the diaper bag, deliberately blanking her mind of all thoughts of the tall, dark, gorgeous man who'd turned her life upside down. Bottles, diapers, a blanket, a pacifier, a sweater and another set of jammies just in case. Good Lord, John probably went out on maneuvers with less equipment.

''And that's another thing,'' Annie said, glancing at her daughter. ''He's not exactly stable right now.'' Jordan blew a spit bubble at her. ''He doesn't know if he's going to stay in the Corps or leave to run his father's company. And if he doesn't even know that, how can he know if he wants to be with us or not?'' Jordan shook her head and waved her arms.

''Don't argue with me, young lady,'' she said in a mock stern voice that brought a flood of giggles rippling from Jordan.

''What's so funny?'' John stepped through the open front door and came across the room in a few lazy strides.

Annie's heartbeat skipped crazily for a long minute as she let herself enjoy the sight of him. Long legs encased in worn blue jeans. A red polo shirt with a Marines emblem right above his heart. Her own heart did a slow roll in her chest despite her best efforts to prevent it. Amazing what that man could do to her simply by walking into a room.

"You ready to go?" John asked as he stepped up behind her and pulled her flush against him.

She closed her eyes and concentrated on the hard, thick strength of his body pressing into hers. Annie swallowed hard and reminded herself to breathe. But it wasn't easy. Not when every time he was near, all she wanted was his hands on her. As if reading her mind, he turned her around in his arms, keeping her close, and slid one hand up to cup her breast.

"Mmmm..." she whispered, and closed her eyes as his thumb and forefinger tweaked and tugged at her nipple. Even through the fabric of her pale-yellow sweater and the bra she wore beneath it, she felt his touch. Right down to her bones.

He bent his head and brushed his lips across hers. "Maybe we don't have to go after all," he whispered, dropping kisses across her forehead, her temples, the bridge of her nose. "Maybe we could stay right here and—"

The baby squawked and kicked her feet against the jumper frame, effectively splintering the mood.

John chuckled, looked over Annie's head at the baby and, smiling, said, "Darlin', you and I are going to have to have a talk about timing."

"Oh," Annie countered, easing back out of his arms and took a deep breath. "I think her timing's excellent."

"Coward," he teased.

"Oh, yeah," she agreed, then tore her gaze from his and busied herself by gathering up Jordan's things. "So," she said, just a little too loudly, "I still think jeans and a sweater is a little underdressed for Easter dinner."

"Not for a backyard barbecue," he told her, stepping around her to pick up the baby.

A barbecue with his family. Well, with his brother Nick and Nick's wife's family. Oh, Lord. "Are you sure it's all right for Jordan and me to come along? I mean, it's a family dinner and everything and—"

He laughed, reached out with one hand to smooth a stray curl back from her face and said, "I keep telling you, Annie. With Italian family gatherings, the more the merrier." Then he paused for a long moment and added, "Besides, you two *are* family."

And thankfully, he turned and headed for the front door before he saw Annie's reaction to his words written all over her face.

Family?

Is that what the three of them were becoming?

And if so, how did she stop it?

But more important, she asked herself desperately, did she *want* to stop it?

Ten

Twilight slipped up on the backyard, stretching shadows along the grass. Annie took a long, deep breath of the cool, ocean-scented air and sat down in one of the dozen or so chairs sprinkled across the Santinis' lawn. It was the first time she'd been alone all day, and though she'd enjoyed herself, it was good to grab at a slice of quiet. If only for a moment or two.

Snatches of conversation and laughter filtered out of the house, where everyone else had gone when Maryann Santini Mazzeo, Gina's mother, had announced she was serving dessert. The brightly lit kitchen practically glowed with life as Annie watched the people streaming back and forth in front of the windows.

She'd never really been around a big family before. And being a part of their ease with each other, the teasing, the bickering, and yes, as John had predicted, the shouting, had been more fun than she had expected.

But at the same time her heart ached just a little for all she'd missed. Her own family never spoke at the dinner table. Meals were simply chores to push through as quickly as possible. Here, she thought with a smile, they were celebrations.

Watching the Santini sisters with their husbands, Annie had felt a sharp tug of envy. Heck, there was so much love in the air in that house a person could get drunk on it.

"A little overwhelming, aren't we?" a deep voice from behind her asked.

Annie turned around in her chair to watch Nick Paretti, John's older brother, approach. He carried ice cream sundaes and handed one to her when he was close enough.

"Thanks," she said, flicking a glance toward the house. "But I should really be going in. See to Jordan."

He chuckled and sat down beside her. "Don't worry about it," he said, and dipped up a spoonful of whipped cream. "Jordan's being passed around like a football in there."

Her eyes went wide, and her fingers tightened on the ice cream bowl.

"It's okay," he said, correctly reading her expression. "The baby's loving the attention, and Gina's mom is in hog heaven."

Maryann Santini Mazzeo, she thought, the older woman's warmth and wide smile rising up in her mind. So different from her own mother, Annie thought with an inward sigh.

"There's nothing Maryann likes better than babies," he was saying, and Annie's attention shifted back to him. "You'd think being a fairly new bride herself, she'd want some time alone with Sal. But then Sal's as bad as she is about the kids."

"It must be nice," Annie said, before she could stop herself.

"What?" He took a bite of the sundae and waited.

"This," she said, waving one hand at the toy-laden yard and the crowded house beyond. "Family. A close family."

"Yeah," he said after a long pause. "Yeah, it is. Though there are times…"

"What times are those, General?" his wife asked as she slipped up behind him, then plopped onto his lap, narrowly missing upsetting his ice cream.

He laughed and gave Annie a "see what I mean?" look. But to Gina, he said only, "Times when I want you all to myself."

"Oh," she retorted, planting a quick kiss on his mouth. "Good answer." Then she turned on his lap and smiled at Annie. "So, when are you and John gonna get married?"

Annie choked on a mouthful of ice cream, and when she had her breath back, she heard Nick saying, "Geez, Gina. Real subtle."

"Who needs subtle?" she asked. "You never find out anything being subtle."

Annie looked around the yard, hoping for a reprieve, but when none came, shifted her gaze back to John's sister-in-law. "We're just friends," she said, and congratulated herself on her quick thinking.

"Uh-huh," Gina said, apparently not convinced. Her gaze still locked on Annie, she said, "Tell me something, Nick, how many women has John brought home to meet the family?"

"None. Gina…"

"Shh…" she said, then leaned forward, smiling at Annie. "Look, I know it's none of my business—"

"But," her husband provided, knowing more was coming.

She ignored him. "*But* anyone can see you're nuts about him."

"You know," Annie said, desperately reaching for a way out of this, "I'd better go check on Jordan and—"

"And John's crazy about you," Gina finished and Annie shut right up and looked at her.

"Gina," Nick said, "keep out of this."

"This is family business and Mama always says, 'Family comes first'." Then, focusing on Annie again, she lowered her voice and said, "I just wanted to put in a good word for the Paretti men, that's all. They make good husbands, and they're really cute."

Well, duh, Annie thought but didn't say. Of course they were cute. Gorgeous, even. But she wasn't in the market for a husband, and John hadn't exactly applied for the job.

"Oh for—" Nick stood up, dragging his buttin-ski wife with him. "Annie, pay no attention to her. She's studying for finals, and the pressure's getting to her."

The screen door swung open, and John stepped onto the porch, with Jeremy Mahoney, Angela's son, and Gina's nephew, right behind him. Nick took a moment to set his ice cream down on the picnic table, then picked up his wife and swung her over his shoulder. Giving her behind a sharp smack with the palm of his hand, he ignored her outraged shriek and said, "We're leaving now. Say goodbye, Gina."

She pushed herself up and grinned. "Goodbye, Gina."

And as her husband started for the house, she called out, "Let's do lunch, okay?"

"Sure," Annie called back as John came up beside her.

He laughed and shook his head as his brother and his wife left the yard and headed for the garage apartment where they were living until Gina graduated from college. "What was that all about?" he asked.

"I'm not really sure," she said, and smiled up at him. It had been a good day. For the first time ever, Annie had felt like part of a family. Sharing baby talk with Marie, though her son Alec was plump and happy and her husband Davis was the picture of a proud father. She'd watched Jeremy scrounge for Easter eggs hidden all over the yard. Laughed at Gina's stories about college and trying to fit in as a Marine wife. She'd been there when Angela had announced to her family that she and Dan were expecting a baby. And she'd realized, as she watched John care for Jordan, that she was, quite hopelessly, in love.

"Are you okay?" John asked, reaching over to touch her cheek gently.

Swirls of wonder rippled along her spine, and Annie had to nod since she couldn't speak with her heart lodged in her throat. Then she did the next best thing. Lifting her hands, she cupped his face and rose up on her toes to plant a quick, hard kiss on his mouth.

He grinned, licked his lips and asked, "What was that for?"

She took a breath and blew it out again, knowing just what she wanted now more than anything else in the world. "It was my way of telling you that I saw the doctor today."

A frown wrinkled his brow.

"Nothing's wrong," she said quickly. "In fact, everything's great. She says I can go back to my regular...activities," she finished, staring into his eyes, willing him to understand.

He did. Comprehension dawned on his features, and as it did, she sensed the tension between them stir to life.

"So," he said tightly, his gaze locked with hers. "You ready to go home now?"

A shiver of anticipation rolled through her with all the subtlety of a Sherman tank. "Oh, yeah."

With the baby asleep in the back seat, John tried like hell to concentrate on his driving. But that wasn't easy. Not with Annie sitting beside him all but vibrating with the same needs crashing through him.

He reached across the gearshift console and laid one hand on her leg. She jumped, then eased back into the seat. John swallowed hard and stroked his palm up and down her thigh, teasing them both with promises of what was to come. And he wished to hell she was wearing a skirt.

The signal up ahead switched from yellow to red, and he brought the car to a stop when everything in him was telling him to hurry.

She laid her hand atop his. He felt her tremble, and the slight sensation swept through him, too. He turned his head to look at her in the weird glow of headlights and traffic lights and he hoped he wasn't reading her expression wrong. She looked so... hungry for him. So eager. His blood pumped ferociously, and when the light turned green again, he didn't notice until the guy behind him laid on the horn.

Nearly growling, he turned his gaze forward, watching the road, steering with one hand while with the other, he explored what he could of her body. Up, up, the length of her thigh to the soft, warm heart of her.

She groaned tightly as he caressed her, and even

through the fabric of her jeans, he felt her heat. Felt her need and shared it. Annie lifted her hips into his touch, fighting against the restraint of the seat belt and the confining clothes.

"Damn," he muttered thickly as the car sped on across town, "I never realized how far away your place is."

"Me, neither," she whispered, and sighed heavily when the next red light stopped them. "Oh, John…"

"Soon, baby," he crooned and slid his hand up to the band of her jeans, knowing he had to touch her. Feel her skin. And he couldn't wait another minute. When she realized what he was up to, she reached to help him. Quickly she undid the snap and zipper, then lifted a bit in her seat to tug her jeans a bit further down.

"Ahh…" He slid his hand down across her abdomen to the very edge of her center and she groaned, trying to move into his touch, trying to feel what they'd both been needing for so long. But the jeans stopped him, and shared frustration shimmered in the air.

"I have to touch you," he whispered, keeping his eyes fixed on the traffic streaming back and forth in front of them.

"I have to feel you," she said just as breathlessly.

He glanced at her. "Take 'em off," he said through gritted teeth.

"My jeans?" she asked, and though she sounded shocked at the thought, he saw a flicker of excitement sparkle in her eyes.

"Yeah. Slide 'em off, Annie."

She shot a hesitant look at the cars alongside them, but no one was paying any attention to them. Turning her gaze back to him, she nodded and unhooked her seat belt.

His mouth went dry as she lifted partially off the seat and tugged her jeans and panties down off her hips. Then, rehooking her seat belt, she used her feet to pull them the rest of the way off.

John looked over at her, half-naked on the seat beside him and he thought he'd die from sheer excitement. It pulsed through him like something alive and fierce inside him.

"I can't believe I'm doing this," she said, and licked dry lips.

"I can't believe we didn't think of this sooner," he said and reached across the seat to touch her.

"Oh, John," she called on a moan, and tipped her head back against the headrest.

Hot and damp and so damn good, he thought, his fingers caressing, exploring. She parted her legs for him, and when the light turned green again, he took off slowly, concentrating on driving, keeping his mind on the flow of traffic while his body was centered on her.

Again and again, he touched her. And Annie stopped worrying about what they were doing. She stopped being shocked. The ripples of excitement fluttering along her spine only sharpened the sensations she experienced. She lifted her hips into his touch and stared blindly out the window, wondering if there were others out there on the road doing the same thing. Wondering if anyone anywhere had *ever* felt what she was feeling. And feeling sorry for everyone who hadn't.

She hardly noticed when he pulled onto her street. Darkness crowded around the car, and the occasional flashes of streetlights ran together in a blurred yellow stream as she concentrated instead on what was happening to her body.

Then he drove the car into her driveway and pulled up alongside her car in the garage. When he shut the engine off and turned to her, she unhooked her seat belt and moved into his embrace. Now, in the shadows, in the darkness, he took her the rest of the way up that peak, and dipping his fingers into her depths, he pushed her over the edge and held her while she fell.

"Get dressed," John said tightly. "And give me your keys. I'll take Jordan in and put her to bed."

Numbly Annie nodded.

John moved quickly, like a man on a mission. And damned if he wasn't. Heavy petting was all well and good, but it was high time they finished what they started.

Carrying the baby into her room, he slipped off her sweater, kissed her forehead, then laid her down gently. Pausing for a moment, he ran his hand along the back of her head and whispered, "I love you, too, you know. Not just your mommy." And as the words slipped out, he knew them for truth. He'd never expected to find love in a mountain cabin. But blast if he hadn't.

Then, smiling to himself, he quietly left Jordan's room, pulling the door to, but not quite closed. Annie came through the front door looking like a refugee. Her pants undone, her sweater wrinkled and her curls standing out in wild array around her head, she only looked at him and said, "Well, are we going to finish this or not?"

"Right after I get back from the drugstore," he told her, already starting for the door.

"No need," she said, stopping him as he walked past her. "I, uh, bought some condoms myself. In case we…you…well—"

He pulled her into his arms and grinned. "After what we just did—in public, mind you—you're embarrassed?"

Annie planted her hands on her hips and cocked her head at him. "Are you going to talk all night or are you going to—"

Then he kissed her and everything else was forgotten in the renewed rush of need pulsing between them. Annie lifted her arms and wrapped them around his neck, and John bent down, scooped her up and carried her to the bedroom. Holding onto her tightly, he freed one arm long enough to swipe all of the pillows off the bed and onto the floor. Then he tossed the quilt to the edge of the bed and laid her down on the mattress.

Her fingers were already tugging at the hem of her sweater when he yanked it off for her. Then as he quickly shucked his clothes, she undid her bra and slid out of her jeans again.

Already hard and ready for her, John snatched up one of the condoms lying on the bedside table and paused just long enough to be grateful she'd planned ahead. Then he ripped the foil packet, sheathed himself and joined her on the bed. Arms lifted, reaching for him, she parted her legs in welcome as he came down to cover her body with his.

His hands moved over her skin with lightning-like flashes of speed and heat. Her breasts, her nipples, her abdomen, the soft cluster of blond curls at the juncture of her thighs. He couldn't touch her enough. Couldn't look enough. Would never be able to satisfy the need to simply *be* with her.

"I can't believe this," she whispered, and arched into his touch.

"What's that?" he asked, his breath brushing her skin as he lavished kisses on her neck, her jaw, her cheek.

"This," she said, her hands sweeping up and down his spine. "I shouldn't be this crazy for you again. So soon after—"

He lifted his head and smiled down at her, and that one dimple flashed wickedly. "Maybe we're both just crazy."

She stroked his cheek with the palm of one hand and asked, "Think they'll lock us up in the same rubber room?"

"If they don't, I'll find a way to get to you."

"Ditto," she murmured as he lowered his head to claim a kiss.

Tongues twisting, breath mingling, they moved together in a fury of touching, tasting, wanting.

And passion soared.

"John," she groaned tightly, as need built within, "now, for heaven's sake, *now*."

"Yes," he whispered, "right now." He couldn't wait another moment, couldn't drag this out any longer. He'd waited for this moment for six long weeks. From the moment he'd met her, he'd known they were headed for this and now he was desperate to be a part of her.

In one swift, sure stroke, he pushed himself home into her heat. Into the depths of her soul and heart, and prayed silently that she'd let him stay there.

A soft moan tore from the back of her throat as he moved at first gently, worried that he might hurt still-tender flesh. But as she rocked into him, wrapping her legs around his hips and drawing him deeper within, he surrendered to the crushing desire choking him.

Again and again he entered and retreated, pushing them both higher, faster. He heard the soft rush of her breath. Felt its warmth on his cheek. Tasted her hunger in the quick, hungry strokes of her tongue and fed his own needs while he gave to her.

Never, he thought wildly as the first stirrings of completion rippled within him, never had he felt so thoroughly at one with someone. This woman, he told himself, was *his*. As he was hers.

Annie's head spun dizzily. Her body alive with sensation, her mind whirled with thoughts of only him. She stared up into his eyes, and in those pale-blue depths, saw a future she wished she was brave enough to claim.

He touched her again—not just her body, but her heart and tears stung the backs of her eyes even as the first ripple of pleasure started deep within her.

She hadn't wanted this. Hadn't counted on it. Hadn't expected it. And now that it was here, she wasn't entirely sure what to do about it.

But then her mind shut down as her body's response to his ministrations took over. Annie shuddered, groaned and moved beneath him, instinct taking over. Need pushing thought aside as she reached for the rush of sensation she knew was hovering just out of reach. She felt it clawing at her, driving her forward. She gloried in the feel of John's body, hard, strong, covering hers, claiming hers.

Then her body exploded into a dazzling burst of light and color and she called his name and held on to him tightly. A moment later he sighed, ''Annie,'' and joined her in a soft, hazy world that belonged to only them.

What could have been hours, but was probably only minutes, passed in stunned silence before she said simply, ''Wow.''

John lifted his head, looked down into her eyes and smiled. ''Definitely worth waiting for.''

''Oh, yeah,'' she agreed. Licking dry lips, she tried to steady her thundering heartbeat, then gave up and let it race. Why shouldn't it? Every nerve ending in her body was jangling. Why should her heart be calm?

Then he moved inside her and her breath caught,

strangling in her throat. It wasn't possible, she thought frantically as her body quickened and came alive again. No way could she be ready for more. Not after what she'd just experienced. "John," she said, shaking her head gently, "I can't. No more. Not yet."

"More," he whispered, dipping his head to taste her lips briefly. "Now," he said and raised up, his body still joined with hers. He ran the flat of his hands up the length of her, stroking her abdomen, cupping her breasts, and when she moaned, he pushed himself deeper inside her. She lifted her hips, moving into him, as if trying to pull him in tighter, closer. He smiled to himself and trailed his fingertips own, across her belly, to the triangle of soft blonde curls at her center. Then he touched her and her body jerked beneath him. He caressed that one small bud of desire until she was writhing beneath him, gritting her teeth, blindly reaching for him.

And desire raged within him. This is what he wanted. This is how he wanted to spend the rest of his life. Loving Annie. Being a part of her, body and soul. And with that knowledge came a hunger to claim her. To make himself such a part of her that she would never want to let him go.

Leaning over her, he rocked his hips and began that long slow climb to completion once again. Her hands came up and encircled his neck. She pulled his head down to hers. Lips met. Breath mingled. Silent promises filled the room and swirled in a thick cloud above them.

And then there was only sensation. Pure, sweet sensation. He gave himself up to the glory of loving her and when he felt her body tense in anticipation of wonder, he plunged inside her again, forcing her up and over the edge of fulfillment, and then following her into the explosive light waiting for them.

Magic, she thought wildly, desperately as her mind and soul splintered. He was magic. What he'd done to her life. What he was doing to her body. It was all magic.

But when the heat slowly drained from her body and she was left cradled in his arms, she thought again, *magic*. And a moment later her traitorous mind clicked on and reminded her that in the end, all magic was merely illusion.

Eleven

"I love you," John said a moment later, and ruined what was left of the afterglow.

Annie inched as far away as she could, which wasn't far enough, considering his body was still locked inside hers. Then she looked straight into his eyes and told him, "No, you don't."

His brow furrowed, his eyes narrowed, and he nearly growled as he said, "What?"

"I said no you don't," she repeated and scooted back while pushing at his chest in a futile attempt to shove him off of her. Naturally, that move didn't work. It was like trying to push a mountain into alignment.

"And you know this how?"

She knew it because she wouldn't allow what she was feeling to be anything else. Annie wasn't prepared to listen to promises of love that would, no doubt, end up being broken. Wasn't it better to never make the promises in the first place?

"It's lust, John," Annie said, ignoring the flash of anger glinting in his eyes. "Now, lust is good, mind you, but it's not love."

"You're not serious."

"Oomph," she grunted as she shoved one more time at him and this time he gave in and rolled to one side of her. She moved, too, as soon as she was able, hoping to keep some distance between them.

"You're darn right I'm serious," she said, swallowing down the knot of regret creeping up her throat.

She had to mean it. She couldn't let herself believe him. Believe *in* him. Annie had believed before, and that had turned out too badly to even think about at the moment. Still, it was that experience that had to guide her actions in this one.

Reaching up, she shoved her hair back from her face, and snatched up the sheet, drawing it high enough that it covered her breasts. Okay, a false sense of security, but right now she was willing to take anything she could get.

John turned the bedside lamp on, and the soft

shadows of evening darted back into the corners of the room. He drew one leg up and rested his forearm atop it. Casually naked and apparently not inclined to cover up, he just stared at her as if her head was on fire.

Her heartbeat thundered in her chest, and the roaring sensation in her ears was deafening. She hadn't expected to be having this conversation tonight. If only he hadn't mentioned the *L* word.

"Quit staring at me," she muttered finally, and told herself not to squirm under his glare. Squirming would look guilty or defensive, and she was neither. Right?

He scraped one hand across his mouth, then slapped the mattress in a burst of frustration. "You know," he said, "I've never said 'I love you' to a woman before tonight."

A quick, all-too-brief spurt of pleasure shot through her before she purposely tamped it down. It didn't—couldn't—matter. Not now. Not ever, she thought, already sensing the loneliness awaiting her during the coming years.

"This isn't exactly the reaction I was expecting."

Okay, now she felt guilty. But then again, she thought, why should she? She hadn't asked him to love her. She hadn't gone out and set a trap and then reeled him in. This had just...*happened.* Now she had to figure out a way to make it *un*happen.

"Look, John," she said, hoping that if she started speaking, the right words would come tumbling out of her mouth. "You can't love me, and I can't love you." There went that hope, she told herself with an inward groan at her less-than-brilliant response.

"Is that right?" he asked, and his voice was a low purr of sound that didn't fool her a bit. He might sound reasonable, but the anger in his tone was unmistakable.

"That's right."

"Care to tell me why?"

"You *know* why," she countered hotly, refusing to have to defend a perfectly logical decision.

What was that old saying? *Burn me once, shame on you. Burn me twice, shame on me?* Well, she'd already been burned, thanks very much, and she wasn't looking for another trip to the emergency room. Oh, she probably never should have slept with him. But after six weeks of being around him, near him, wanting him...well, she was only human, right?

"Because of Jordan's father?" he asked, incredulity coloring his voice.

"Well," she said, swinging her tumbled hair back from her eyes again, "give the Marine a prize." Then she turned and half fell off the bed, dragging the sheet with her. She took a step, stumbled and righted herself again before wrapping the fabric around her like an ivy-patterned toga. Then, lifting her chin, she sniffed once, clutched at her sheet and said, "Bingo, big boy. Mike Sinclair might not have been good for much, but he was a good teacher."

When John opened his mouth to argue, she rushed right on before he could start.

"He taught me well, John. He made promises, told me pretty lies, then got me pregnant and disappeared." She forced herself to look into his eyes, figuring she owed him at least that much. "He said he loved me, too. Didn't stop him from leaving."

"So, naturally," John said slowly, too calmly, as he slid off the bed and turned to face her, "that means *I'm* a bastard, too."

"You're a man," she pointed out, unnecessarily, she thought, with a quick glance down his unmistakably male body. Oh, boy.

"Guilty as charged," he told her tightly.

"And I'm not looking for a man."

"Too bad, since you found one, anyway."

Had she ever. Too bad she couldn't keep him. "John, you don't have to make this so hard."

Shaking his head, he stalked across the room, covering the distance between them in a few long strides. Then he grabbed her shoulders in a firm grip and gave her a quick shake. "Are you nuts?" Astonishment shone in his eyes, along with an anger that darn near set fire to her skin. "I'm going to make this as hard as I can."

"Why?" she countered, jerking out of his grasp and backing up until the windowsill nudged at the backs of her thighs. "What's the point? Why beat each other up over something that won't change?"

"What's the point?" he repeated. "I *love* you, that's the point."

Annie took a deep breath and told herself not to listen. Not to hear the thread of panic in his voice. Not to surrender to her own heart, which was telling her to forget the past and fling herself at him. How could she trust a heart that was so easily fooled?

"You're punishing me—*us*—for the actions of some other guy. An incredibly *stupid* guy."

"I'm not punishing you," she snapped, wanting to believe it. "I'm protecting myself. And Jordan."

"I love that baby," he told her. "Like she was my own. And you damn well know it."

A sheen of tears unexpectedly filled her eyes, and she blinked them back. Darn it, yes. She did know it. She saw it every time he picked Jordan up. Every time he smiled at her. And maybe one day Jordan would resent her mother for throwing away her best chance at a real daddy.

But wasn't it a mother's duty to protect her child

the best way she knew how? And that's all Annie was doing, blast it.

"Yes," she said, realizing she had to give him this, at least. "I know you love her."

He nodded.

"Today."

He tensed and took a step closer. Annie edged to one side. Not that she was afraid of him. She was only worried that if he got his hands on her again, she might surrender. Give in to what her body and her heart were telling her to do. "But who knows what tomorrow will bring?" she demanded.

"You're right," he said. "None of us knows what tomorrow's going to bring. Isn't that the whole point of enjoying what you have while you have it?"

"I *have* to think about tomorrow," she told him and felt a soft, ocean breeze dance beneath the partially opened window and sail past her. "I have Jordan's future to consider. Her happiness."

"And I want to be a part of that future," he said, slamming both hands at his bare, narrow hips.

But she wouldn't be swayed. Couldn't allow herself to be. So she dragged out her last weapon and fired it. "You don't even know what you're going to do with your *own* future."

"What?"

"You told me you love being a Marine."

"Yeah, so?"

"So, you're willing to turn your back on what you love to go and sell computers." He winced, and she kept on going. "You tell me to follow my heart," she told him, "but are you?"

"That's different."

"No, it's not," she told him. "I know what being a Marine means to you, and you're going to give it up, just like that." And she snapped her fingers.

"I *owe* my father," he ground out.

Annie took a step toward him and looked up into his eyes. "Bull. When Jordan grows up, she won't *owe* me anything."

John reached up and shoved both hands along the side of his head, wishing for the first time in years he had enough hair to pull out in frustration. "You don't understand."

"Oh, yeah, I do," she said. "You're giving up what you love for something else. Just like one day you would give *me* up for something or some*one* else."

How in the hell was a man supposed to fight an illogical, irrational argument like that one? He looked into those deep-blue eyes of hers and saw that she meant every word. Believed everything she'd just said. Frustration gave way to pure anger. Damn it, he didn't deserve her distrust.

"Besides," she snapped, marching around the

room like some curly-headed Cleopatra in a toga, "your father doesn't need you to leave the Corps to run that company. Any halfwit could run it from a laptop anywhere in the world."

"Is that right?" he countered, not really caring, but getting caught up in her speech.

"That's right. All he needs is to simplify. Install a faster modem, get a more user-friendly Internet page...."

John's mind blanked out as it often did when people drifted into computer speak. But even he could see that she was on a tear, rattling off one idea after another. Though they made little sense to him, he had a feeling his father would have been impressed.

When she finally ran down, she turned on him. "Why in heaven's name your father would want any of you to be in charge of a company none of you care a fig about is beyond me."

"We're family," he said simply, knowing that those two words said it all.

"Family," she repeated, wrapping her arms around herself in an age-old defensive posture.

John felt his heart drop at the closed-off look in her eyes and knew that whatever she said next he wasn't going to like.

He was right.

"Well," Annie said, lifting her chin again in a

gesture he was really too fond of, "Jordan and I are a family now, too. And the two of us will get along just fine."

"Damn it, Annie," he said, taking a step closer, and stopping again when she shook her head firmly.

"Just…go, okay?"

"Not until this is settled."

She shoved her hair back from her eyes, met his gaze squarely, so that he was in no doubt about the tears glittering across the surface of those blue depths, then she said, "It *is* settled, John."

She was locking him out. Pushing him out of the circle of warmth he'd found here in this small apartment. Well, he'd go. For now. But he'd be back, too.

Because no Paretti alive had ever given up on anything important to him…or her. And he wasn't about to be the first. But at the same time it was clear he wouldn't get through to her tonight. What he needed was a battle plan. And some time to make it work.

"Okay," he said, and saw shock flicker in her eyes briefly. Well, good. At least he could still surprise her. "I'll go."

Was that disappointment he saw flash across her features? It was gone so quickly he couldn't be sure, but John clung to it, anyway. She just stood in the doorway watching him as he quickly threw his clothes on. Hard to believe that a night that had started out so well had ended so badly, he thought grimly.

In a few seconds he was dressed and facing her, and it took every ounce of control he possessed to keep his voice even when he said, "This isn't over, Annie. I won't let it be."

"You don't get a vote here, John."

"That's where you're wrong, honey," he told her, and swept her up into his arms. Dipping his head, he kissed her. Long and hard and hot and deep, he poured every bit of his love into that kiss and silently demanded that she accept it. When her arms encircled his neck and held on, he mentally declared a victory.

This war wasn't over. Not by a long shot.

And with that thought firmly in mind, he released her abruptly. She staggered backward into the door, and he marched past her, straight through the hall and the living room and out the front door.

Let her miss him. By damn, she'd *better* miss him.

One week crawled into two and Annie wasn't over him yet.

Irritating but true. She'd tried everything she could think of. She'd watched old movies and cried herself to sleep. She'd eaten enough ice cream to sink a battleship. She'd stared at the phone, willing it to ring and then cursing it when it did.

In short, she'd used every weapon in the "getting over a man" arsenal, and it wasn't helping.

It was beginning to appear that there would be no getting over John Paretti.

Heck, even her dreams were filled with images of him. Night after night she tossed and turned, haunted by the memory of his voice, his touch, his kiss. And morning after morning, she awoke, alone and incredibly aroused. It just wasn't fair, she thought, stabbing at a particularly stubborn weed in the flower bed. Before John, she'd had no trouble living without sex.

Now, though, now that she knew what it could be like between a man and a woman, now that she craved his touch, she was forced back into celibacy.

Beside her on the lawn, Jordan giggled.

"Sure," Annie muttered, glancing at her daughter, "easy for you to laugh."

Still, it wasn't just the sex she missed. It was the laughter. The times spent together on the couch, watching a movie. It was fighting over the buttered popcorn, sharing excitement over each of Jordan's accomplishments, washing the car and having a water fight.

"Hard to have a water fight by yourself," she muttered and leaned back on her heels. Her shoulders hurt, her knees were aching, but half the flower bed looked decent again. At least she'd accomplished *something*. She certainly hadn't gotten much work done.

And even winning the contract with the diaper company hadn't been as satisfying as it should have been, because John hadn't been there to share in it.

"He's doing this on purpose, you know," Annie told Jordan, and her daughter looked at her through wide blue eyes as if asking what in the heck she was talking about. So Annie explained. "He's staying away on purpose. Making me miss him. He thinks it'll drive me so crazy being without him that I'll give in and call." She waved her trowel in the air like a sword. "But he's wrong. I won't call. And I won't miss him. Not anymore."

Jordan blew a spit bubble, telling her mother quite plainly what she thought of that statement.

"Okay, so I will miss him. But I'll get over it. Eventually." Sighing, she added, "Shouldn't take more than another twenty or thirty years."

From inside the apartment the phone rang, and Annie reacted like a firehouse dog. Snatching up the baby, she sprinted for the porch, taking the steps two at a time. Flinging open the screen door, she paused long enough to lay Jordan down in the playpen before racing for the phone, now on its third impatient ring.

"Casual," she told herself breathlessly. "Be casual." She picked up the receiver. "Hello?" There. Warm. Friendly. Casual.

"Anne?" the female voice on the other end inquired through a burst of static. "Is this Anne Foster?"

Annie sighed and leaned against the kitchen counter, trying to fight off a wave of disappointment. "Yes, Mother, it's me."

"That should be *I*, dear," the woman corrected.

"Whatever," Annie muttered, then louder asked, "How are you and Father?"

"We are both in the best of health, Anne. Your father sends his hellos."

Hellos, not his love, Annie thought and wondered when she would ever stop hoping they would change. And a little voice inside reminded her that someone else had offered her love just a couple of weeks ago and she'd thrown it right back in his face.

Ironic, huh?

"I'm calling to let you know that we won't be home this summer after all."

The static rattled terribly, and Annie moved around the kitchen, futilely hoping to fix the connection. But her mother kept talking and by the time it was clear, all Annie heard was "...a fascinating discovery, really."

"That's wonderful," she said, because she knew it was expected.

"What's that?"

"I said, that's wonderful, Mother."

"Ah," her mother said, apparently out of conversation. "Well then, I'll call again next month."

Annie gripped the phone more tightly and shouted to be heard over the growing disruption on the line. "I had the baby, mother," she said, knowing her mother wouldn't have been keeping track of such minor things as the birth of her first granddaughter. "A little girl. Jordan's beautiful."

"Well how nice, dear. I'm sure your father will be pleased." The line popped, hummed and then sputtered on her mother's last words. "We'll be in touch."

Then Annie was holding a phone listening to nothingness. Useless, ridiculous tears spilled over the edge of her eyes and rolled unheeded down her cheeks. One more time, she thought, feeling the pain of knowing she didn't matter to the two people she should have mattered to most. With shaking hands, she hung up the phone and walked into the living room, where Jordan lay on her back, studiously examining her toes.

Dropping to the floor beside the playpen, Annie looked in at her daughter and wished she could have given her sweet baby the family, the father she deserved. But she'd had her chance, her heart whispered, and Annie felt a new, sharper pain replace the old ache.

John had offered her his love, and she'd turned him down. She hadn't trusted him or herself, and now he was gone. She couldn't fool herself anymore. He wasn't going to call. He wouldn't be dropping by. She was alone. Just her and her baby—and thinking anything else would simply be giving in to fantasy. She'd been stupid. And so damned foolish.

And she was realizing it all too late.

Unless—

She came up on her knees, brushed the backs of her hands across her cheeks to wipe away the tears and looked in at Jordan. "What do you think? Should I call him?"

The baby gurgled something nonsensical that sounded like an agreement to Annie. So before she could change her mind or chicken out or logic herself out of this, she got up and hurried back to the kitchen.

There on a pad beside the phone was the number John had left for her. Snatching up the receiver, she swallowed her pride and dialed the number.

"Staff Sergeant Jackson," a male voice announced after the first ring.

"Peter?"

"Annie? Hey, how you doing? Lisa's been wanting to get you and the baby over for dinner and—"

"Soon," she said. "Is John around? I mean, is he too busy to talk to me for a minute?"

A long pause ticked past, and she wondered if John was standing there in the office, coaching his friend into lying to her on his behalf. Finally, though, Peter said, "Uh, Annie, John's in Florida. Didn't you know?"

Her heart sank. Funny, she'd read that description in countless books and never really knew what it meant. Now, she knew all too well. A black hole opened up at her feet, and she felt herself slipping into it. "No," she said numbly. "No, I didn't."

"Geez, honey, I thought sure he would've told you. His dad had a heart attack."

She closed her eyes and leaned back against the wall. He'd had a family crisis and he hadn't called to tell her. To let her offer to help. "Is he—"

"He's all right. Hell, it'd take an act of God to kill a Paretti."

She was pretty sure a heart attack *was* an act of God, but that wasn't the point, now was it? The point was, John had obviously done what he'd said he was going to do. He'd left the Corps. He'd gone to Florida to run the Paretti Computer Corporation. And he'd left her behind without so much as a goodbye.

"Annie?" Peter asked, and his voice sounded far away, buried beneath the thundering in her ears. "Are you okay?"

"I'm fine," she said, and hoped to heaven her friend believed the lie. Then she added, "Say hi to Lisa for me, all right? Bye, Peter."

"Sure," he answered, "talk to you soon."

Carefully, deliberately, she hung up the phone, severing her last connection with John Paretti. Then, her back braced against the wall, she slid down, down, until she was sitting on the cold, linoleum floor. Drawing her legs up, she wrapped her arms around them and buried her face there.

And John's face rose to the surface of her mind, and she clung to it like a life raft tossed into a churning sea.

Twelve

"What do you mean, you don't want the job?"

John stared at his father's flushed face and fought down a stab of guilt. Hell, the old man had only just survived what his doctor was referring to as a wake-up call. The mild heart attack hadn't been enough to put the fear of God into Dominick Paretti, but it had given him some pretty strong ammunition. And he wasn't above using it now.

The old man laid one hand on his desk and opened the other against his chest, grimaced tightly and sent John a glance from beneath half-lowered eyelids. When he saw that his youngest son wasn't panicking, he let his hand drop to the arm of the chair and dropped the pretense as well. "Even a heart attack's not enough to get you back here to help out, eh?"

Ah, guilt. His parents' preferred weapon of choice. And damned if they didn't fire it accurately.

"I'm here, aren't I?" John asked, and took a seat opposite his father's desk.

"Yeah," Dom said on a sigh as he pulled open the bottom right drawer of his desk, "but you're not staying."

He'd planned to, John thought. He really had. Figured that his father's heart attack was a sign, telling him that he should leave the Corps. Run the family business.

But then on the flight to Florida, he'd had time to think. And when he'd arrived to find his father already recovering and as ornery as usual, he'd done even more thinking. Now that the trouble was past and his brothers had gone back to their homes, John was still here, taking another week or so of personal leave to sort things out.

And the simple truth of the matter was, Annie was right. She'd accused him of not following his own advice, and damned if she didn't have a point. His heart would never be in the computer industry. He was a soldier, a professional military man, and that's how he liked it. His life was built around the

Marines, and changing it would only make him—
and anyone around him—miserable.

"No," he said softly as he watched his father
pull a bottle of bourbon from the drawer and set it,
along with a couple of glasses onto the desk. "I'm
not. And you're not supposed to be drinking."

Dom shrugged, pulled open the top drawer and
dug out two cigars. Handing one to his son, he kept
the other and clipped the end off. "It's not the bourbon and cigars that brought that twinge on."

"It wasn't a twinge," John told him, leaning forward to accept a light, "it was a heart attack."

"Angina."

"Same thing."

"Christ, who's the father here?" Dom asked, and
leaned back in his chair. Puffing on the cigar, he
smiled to himself, then waved a hand at the bottle.
"Maybe it's just as well you're not staying. Bad
enough I have to hear lectures from your mother.
Damned if I'll take 'em from you."

"You don't listen to anybody," John told him.
"Never have."

"Then we're a lot alike now, aren't we?" Dom
asked, one dark eyebrow lifting. Then he looked at
his youngest son for a long minute before saying,
"Pour us a drink, son. You look like you've got
something to say that'll go down a lot easier with
aged whiskey."

Late-afternoon sunlight peeked between the folds of the curtains hanging across the wide window overlooking the front yard. Dust motes danced in the sliver of light that played along the spines of the books lining the walls in tall shelves. It was a man's room, John thought, and knew his mother probably never ventured into Dom's inner sanctum. Which was, no doubt, why the older man felt completely safe indulging in his favorite vices.

Sighing to himself, John surrendered and poured each of them a short drink, splashing the amber liquid into crystal glasses. When he passed one to his father, he shook his head as the old man tossed the liquor down his throat in one gulp.

Dom saw the expression on his son's face and muttered, "Don't look so damn grim. Crisis over."

"This time."

"Hey, nobody lives forever."

"Great attitude."

"You know," Dom said, shifting to lean both forearms on his desk, "if I wanted another lecture, I could just call your mother in here and have done with it. So how about you just say what you have to say."

"I already did," he said. "I'm not staying. I can't take over the company."

"Don't suppose it'd help if I clutched at my chest and moaned?"

Had to give the old man credit. "No," he said, smiling, "it wouldn't."

"Yeah," Dom muttered. "Didn't work with your brothers, either. Bunch of hardheads, the lot of you."

"Wonder where we got it?"

The older man smiled slightly.

"You don't need me, Dad. You need someone who knows computers. Someone with ideas for the company's growth," he reached into his memory for everything Annie had shouted at him just a week or so ago. "Like installing faster modems, building a more user-friendly Internet home page..."

Dom leaned in and gave his son a narrow-eyed, suspicious stare.

So John kept talking. In a few minutes he'd rattled off every idea Annie had had. At least, the ones he could remember. And as he looked at his father, he knew he had Dom's attention.

The old man tapped his fingers along the edge of the ox-blood leather desk blotter until the tapping sounded like the drum section of the Corps band. Finally, though, he stopped, tilted his head to one side and looked at his son. "Thought you said you didn't know anything about the business."

"I don't," John said, leaning forward himself. "But I know someone who does."

"This is a *family* company," his father reminded him.

"She'll meet that criterion soon enough," John told his father, hoping to hell he'd be able to convince Annie once he got hold of her again.

"Is that right?"

A gleam of interest sparked in Dom's eyes and John knew he had him. Nothing the old man liked better than fresh ideas and someone to talk about them with.

"So who is this computer wizard?"

"Her name's Annie..."

Summer was just around the corner. Already the days were getting warmer and longer. The kids in the neighborhood were out on their skateboards, and the older ones were strapping their surfboards into their car racks.

The ocean breeze winding its way down the narrow street carried the scent of summer on it and seemed to be enticing everyone to come to the beach. From her spot on the tree-shaded front lawn, Annie paused in her weed pulling to ease back and watch the Hollis kids from across the street playing catch with their dad.

A small nudge of regret poked at her heart as she tore her gaze from her neighbors to look at Jordan, lying on the quilt beside her. The baby was so big now. So much her own person. At three months old, Jordan was wide-eyed and interested in everything. What would she be like at three years? At thirteen? Would she still be happy? Would she miss having a father?

She certainly wouldn't have any memories of the man who'd loved her so much. And that didn't seem fair. Or right. John Paretti had stormed into their lives in the nick of time. And just like a fairy-tale Prince Charming, he'd been there whenever they'd needed him.

And then, rather than acting like the princess in the story, Annie had turned into a wicked witch on him. She'd closed the door on a future, thrown his declaration of love back into his face and sentenced herself and Jordan to a life without him.

"I really screwed up, sweetie," Annie said, and dusted her hands together, getting rid of most of the dirt. "You love him. I love him. And I let him walk away—no, I did worse than that. I ran him off."

Jordan gurgled and Annie kept talking. Not that she was saying anything new here. She'd been telling herself these same things for the past few weeks. Every day that passed and the phone didn't ring. Every time the mailman didn't deliver a letter from John. Every time she drove past the gates of Camp Pendleton.

She'd had it all, and she'd been too stupid to see

it. And why? Because she'd assumed John was no better than Mike Sinclair. She'd condemned him on no evidence, mind you. Just the fact that they were both men. Well, male, at any rate, since John Paretti was three times the man Jordan's father had been.

Too bad she hadn't realized that in time.

"You know," she said aloud, considering, "we could always fly to Florida. Go visit John. Talk to him. If he doesn't throw Mommy out of his office. Maybe if I just went to him, told him that I love him, maybe—"

"It's worth a shot," a deep voice from directly behind her said.

Jordan giggled, one of those deep-down from the belly giggles that only babies seemed to have mastered.

"John?" Annie pivoted on one knee and watched him approach, smiling. And, oh, boy, did he look good in his uniform. Her heart thundered in her chest, her throat tightened and still she managed to squeeze out two words. "You're here," she said, unnecessarily.

"Came straight from the airport," he told her, dropping his duffel bag onto the lawn. His gaze shifted toward the baby, then back to Annie. She almost *felt* his stare, like a touch. It had been so long, she thought. And it had almost been forever.

She didn't know why he'd come back. Didn't want to look a gift horse in the mouth.

Didn't want to waste what might be her last chance.

"I'm so glad you're here," she said, standing up and brushing at the dirt clinging to her knees. Wouldn't you know that when she saw him again she'd be sweaty and dirty from the garden? Ah, well, she wouldn't let opportunity's knock go unanswered again.

"Are you?"

"Oh, yeah," she assured him, as she silently pleaded with the butterflies in her stomach to take a seat. "But I'm sort of surprised, too. Peter told me you went to Florida. That your dad had had a heart attack."

"All true."

"How is he?"

"Cranky as ever," John said with a smile.

"I'm glad."

"Thanks."

Well, she thought, this was going nicely. They'd talked more in the first few minutes when they'd met. Although she had been throwing a lamp at him at the time.

Where were all her brave ideas now, huh? She'd been longing for the chance to talk to him. To tell him that she'd been stupid and cowardly. That she loved him and wanted him. That she wanted them—the three of them—to be a family.

And now that she had the chance, her tongue felt too thick to form the words.

"I had to see you," John said, breaking the silence between them, for which Annie was grateful.

"You did?"

"Yeah," he said, bracing his legs wide apart and folding his arms across a chest that looked even broader than she remembered. "I've got a job offer for you."

"A *job?*" she repeated, feeling twin peaks of disappointment and anger jab at her insides. This is why he'd come to her? About a job? She'd been missing him, realizing she loved him and he wanted to hire her for some dumb job?

Her own fault, Annie thought. She'd taken his love and tossed it. John was a proud man. No way would he come back and give her a second chance to brush him aside. Nope. Now it was up to her to win him back.

"I don't care about the job," she said, taking a step toward him.

One black eyebrow lifted. "You don't?"

"Uh-uh." She shook her head, then pushed her hair out of her eyes with one grubby hand. "When I found out you went to Florida without even saying goodbye…"

"There wasn't time," he said.

"That's when I realized something I should have known all along," she said, interrupting him and not caring. "I love you, John. I didn't mean to. I didn't want to. And God knows," she added with a strained laugh, "I'd be a lot less scared if I didn't love you—"

"I hear a *but* coming," he said, watching her through wary eyes.

"*But*," she said, "I'd be a lot less alive, too."

One corner of his mouth quirked into a half smile, but he didn't say a word. He just waited.

She couldn't blame him. He'd already proclaimed himself, and she hadn't exactly greeted that proclamation with open arms.

"I love you," she said again, relishing how the words felt on her tongue, hoping he would believe her. Hear the truth in her voice, see it in her eyes. She'd never thought to say those words again in her life, and the fact that she was being given the opportunity was the greatest gift she'd ever received. "Jordan loves you. We missed you so much when you were gone. *I* missed you so much. We weren't complete anymore without you. And we don't ever want to lose you again. So I guess what I'm saying is, we want to marry you."

At last she'd surprised him. She saw it in his

expression, and she took heart in the gleam of hope she saw shining in his eyes.

"You do, huh?"

"We do," she said firmly. "We want to marry you and move to Florida and help you with the family business and we want to have more babies. We want to be a family. A *real* family."

"And what if I'm not running the family business?" he asked, reaching out to stroke one hand down the length of her arm.

"Huh?" She blinked up at him. "But you went to Florida—you said that you were going to leave the Corps and—"

"I know what I said," John told her, his voice tight with the want that had brought him here as soon as his plane had touched ground at Orange County Airport. "But I did some thinking, too."

"Yeah?" she asked, stepping up closer still, laying her hand on his chest. He felt warm for the first time in weeks.

"Yeah." John swallowed hard, laid both hands on her shoulders and promised himself to never let go again. A soft ocean breeze ruffled her hair, stirring the curls into a dance about her dirt-streaked face. She'd never looked more beautiful to him than she did at this moment. "You were right, you know."

"About what?" Her gaze moved over his features and he caught the sheen of unshed tears in those lake-blue depths.

"About me taking my own advice. I told you to follow your heart, but I wasn't listening to my own." He shook his head slowly and smiled just a little. "I'm no business man. Not even for my father can I leave the Corps. I have to be who I am—or I'm no good to anyone."

She lifted one hand and touched his cheek. "Who you are is plenty. For anyone."

"I was hoping you'd say that."

She grinned. "I asked you to marry me, didn't I?"

He smiled back at her. "So you did."

"Are you going to answer that question anytime soon, Gunnery Sergeant Paretti?"

"After you tell me if you're interested in that job offer I was telling you about."

She took a breath and huffed it out again in frustration. "You want to talk about a job? Now? In the middle of my proposal?"

"Yep." God, it felt good to be back with her. Where he belonged.

"Fine," she said, waving one hand at him. "What job?"

"Running Paretti Computer Corporation."

She staggered backward a step, stared up at him

through huge, astonished eyes and gasped, "What?"

"You heard me," he said on a laugh and caught her to him when she staggered again. "The old man loved your ideas—"

"What ideas?"

"The ones you rattled off at me when you were yelling at me to follow my heart."

"You can't be serious," she said, shaking her head.

"Oh, yes, I can," he said, enjoying the fact that he'd been able to surprise her just as she had him with that proposal. She'd gone and wrecked his carefully rehearsed, romantic-as-hell proposal speech, but, remembering her words to him, he figured it was worth it.

"But—"

"No buts," he cut her off quickly, pulled her tightly to him and wrapped his arms around her, keeping her from escaping, even if she'd wanted to, which she didn't. "So, you tell me if you want the job, then I'll tell you if I'll marry you."

"You're crazy, you know that?" she said, stunned disbelief coloring her tone.

"That's been said before."

"And will be again, no doubt."

"Oh," he said with a grin, "no doubt."

Her arms came around his waist and her palms

splayed wide on his back. He felt the warmth of each of her fingers all the way down to his soul, and John knew he'd found his home. His heart.

"So—" he prodded gently with a little squeeze "—do you want the job?"

Annie told herself that if John came with the job, she'd sign up to sweep streets on Jupiter. But he hadn't actually *said* he came with the job now, had he? "Sure, I guess so, I mean—"

"Then I guess I'll have to say yes to your proposal and marry you," he said with a wink, "since this *is* a family-run company after all."

The last of her reservations drained away, leaving her feeling like an exceptionally lucky woman. "Very sneaky," she said smiling. "I like that in a man."

"I aim to please," he said, bending his head to plant a kiss on her neck.

"Mmm…" she moaned, and added, "…then aim a little lower, okay?"

"Aye-aye, ma'am," he whispered, sliding his lips down, along her collarbone and then back up to claim a kiss that sealed their promises and blessed their future.

Epilogue

Three Years Later...

Green and white balloons dropped from the netting overhead and spilled down onto the gleaming wooden floor where dozens of couples were dancing to a ballad from the forties. But Annie's gaze was locked on one couple in particular.

Her handsome husband and their three-year-old daughter, dancing cheek to cheek. John held Jordan tightly and moved into a series of spins that had the little girl laughing in delight, and Annie's heart blossomed painfully in her chest.

So much, she thought, letting her gaze stray just a bit to wander across the faces of the gathered crowd. She'd found so much in three short years. A man who was husband, lover and friend. A career that just kept getting better. And a family.

The family she'd always wanted and given up hoping to find.

She smiled to herself as she spotted Sam and Karen, chasing their two-year-old, Anthony, across the floor. Then grinned when she spotted Nick hovering over a *very* pregnant Gina as if she might explode. And, she told herself as her gaze moved on, in the heart of the family was Dominick and Teresa Paretti, the couple whose fiftieth anniversary they were all here to celebrate.

They danced together now in the center of the floor, and the crowd parted, making way. Amid the swirling lights, the sea of balloons and their watchful audience, the Parettis had eyes only for each other.

And Annie sighed.

"Tired?" John's voice came from right beside her, and she turned, smiling, to face him.

"Not a bit," she said.

"Mommy, Daddy says I'm the prettiest girl here," Jordan piped up from her perch on John's hip.

"And he's absolutely right," Annie told her, leaning in for a kiss.

"Well," John amended solemnly, "except for your mommy."

The look in his eyes sent a dart of heat shooting through her, and Annie had to marvel at it. Three years married, eight months pregnant with her second child, and one look from her husband turned her into a puddle of steaming want.

Jordan nodded, sending her thick, honey-colored braids flying. "'Cept for Mommy."

John kept his gaze locked with hers, and after a long minute he set Jordan on her feet and said, "Why don't you go dance with Uncle Nick? He looks lonely."

"'Kay," the child announced and skipped off toward her next conquest.

"That was sneaky," Annie said, moving into his arms and swaying in time with the music.

"Hey, I needed a minute alone with my best girl...." He shot a look over at Gina who looked relieved when Nick and Jordan moved into the dancing crowd. "And Gina could use a break from my big brother."

"He's worried," Annie said. "She's due any day now."

"I know," John told her laughing. "I already told him that it was no problem. If Gina goes into labor, I'm completely ready to deliver their little boy. It's not like I haven't done it before.''

Annie laughed and shook her head. ''Gee, and that didn't make him feel better?''

He grinned down at her. ''Nope.'' Then he moved one hand to stroke the mound of her stomach. ''But I guess I can't blame him. When our new little miss decides to make her entrance, I think I'd prefer having a doctor there.''

''We still don't have a name for her,'' Annie said.

''I wanted to talk to you about that,'' he told her, and guided her into a slow turn, ''I'd like to name her Faith, if that's okay with you.''

''Faith Paretti,'' she murmured, staring straight up into her husband's eyes. ''Has a nice ring to it.''

''Has a nice sound, too,'' he said softly, his gaze moving over her features like the most gentle of caresses. ''Faith in us. Faith in the future. Faith in all we have together.''

Tears stung the backs of her eyes, and Annie blinked them away. Everything about this man touched her heart so deeply. She couldn't imagine her life without him. And thank heaven, she would never have to. ''Faith it is, then,'' she said.

John watched her for a long minute and felt his heart fill to bursting. His wife. The mother of his children. The other half of his heart.

She was all those things and so much more.

He'd found a happiness he hadn't thought possible. And it was all due to this one woman. The woman who made his life complete.

Absently he noted that the orchestra had stopped playing and that the crowd was beginning to move through the French doors toward the dock. It must be time for the fireworks display, he thought, never taking his gaze from Annie's.

"John," she said softly.

"Hmm?"

"We should go and join the family."

"Yeah," he murmured, "I suppose we should."

"The fireworks are about to start."

John ran one hand up and down her spine, bent to kiss her gently, briefly, then lifted his head and looked at her. "Honey, the fireworks are right here. Trust me."

Then he kissed her, and Annie could have sworn she saw the flash of a brightly colored rocket explode behind her closed eyes.

*   *   *   *   *

Look for more books in Maureen Child's

BACHELOR BATTALION

series later in 2001,
only from Silhouette Desire.

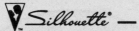

SILHOUETTE® MAKES YOU A STAR!

Look in the back pages of
all June Silhouette series books to find an
exciting new contest with fabulous prizes!
Available exclusively through Silhouette.

Don't miss it!

Silhouette®

Where love comes alive™

P.S. Watch for details on how you can meet
your favorite Silhouette author.

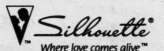

Desire®

January 2001
TALL, DARK & WESTERN
#1339 by Anne Marie Winston

February 2001
THE WAY TO A RANCHER'S HEART
#1345 by Peggy Moreland

March 2001
MILLIONAIRE HUSBAND
#1352 by Leanne Banks
Million-Dollar Men

April 2001
GABRIEL'S GIFT
#1357 by Cait London
Freedom Valley

May 2001
THE TEMPTATION OF
RORY MONAHAN
#1363 by Elizabeth Bevarly

June 2001
A LADY FOR LINCOLN CADE
#1369 by BJ James
Men of Belle Terre

MAN
OF THE
MONTH

MAN OF THE MONTH

For twenty years Silhouette has been giving
you the ultimate in romantic reads. Come join
the celebration as some of your favorite authors
help celebrate our anniversary with the most
sensual, emotional love stories ever!

Available at your favorite retail outlet.

Silhouette®
Where love comes alive™

Visit Silhouette at www.eHarlequin.com   SDMOM01